Captive in the Quonset Hut
A Kate and Doris Mystery

by

Trisha Durrant

For information, email Cozy Cat Press, cozycatpress@aol.com or visit our website at: www.cozycatpress.com

COZY CAT
P R E S S

ISBN: 978-1-946063-78-6
Printed in the United States of America

10 9 8 7 6 5 4 3 2 1

To Kristy, Tammy, John and Gwen. I couldn't do it without you and my amazing grandchildren, Erica, Diane, Briana, Garrett, Kelsey, Hanna, Shamaine and Jayden.

Prologue

The young woman shivered. It was cold. She was lying on something soft but it didn't feel like her own bed. A thin scratchy blanket covered her, not her silky duvet. She put her hand up to her face. Her nose and cheeks were icy. *Maybe the frosty air was the reason the pain in her head was getting worse, but why did her brain seem to be wrapped in a thick fog and what was that nasty odor?* She struggled to remember and finally recognized the smell—*mold, the blanket smelled like mold.*

She tried to get up but there was something heavy around her leg that prevented it. After three attempts she struggled into a sitting position. A wave of nausea swept over her. She closed her eyes tightly and took deep breaths until the feeling eventually passed.

After a time, she didn't know how long, she slowly opened them. By the light seeping in around the door, she saw that she was lying on a mattress on the floor of an old metal building. It was a familiar shape. *Where had she had seen it before?* The pounding in her head made coherent thought difficult but she knew this structure. The walls were of corrugated metal, the ceiling arched and it had a specific name. Finally it came to her, *World War II History—Quonset hut. What did the book say?—Easily erected and transportable.*

But where was she and how did she get here? The last thing she remembered was being in class. *No, there was something after that, but what?* It was important, but she didn't remember why. There was a cup of water on the floor next to the mattress. She reached for it and greedily gulped it down. Her eyes slowly closed and she sank back into the black void.

It was much later when she awoke. There was no light showing around the door of her prison. The last time she was conscious she thought it to be morning. If she were correct, by the darkness it could be as much as ten hours later—maybe more. She was thirsty and there was a fresh cup of water next to her makeshift bed. She picked it up.

A rattling noise alerted her. Someone was outside the door. There was the sound of a chain being drawn through a hasp. She pulled down the blanket and poured the water over the front of her jeans, tossed the cup away and pulled the blanket back over her. Every nerve in her body was vibrating. *I have to be calm. I have to think.* She slowed her breathing to give the impression she was still in a deep sleep.

Footsteps came across the floor. Someone knelt down next to her. She heard the cracking of their knees. A hand came out and gently stroked the side of her face. It took every ounce of self control to not shudder. She heard the sound of water being poured into her cup and smelled food. Whoever it was slid their hand beneath her blanket, but recoiled when it encountered the wet jeans. She heard a disgusted snort. *Male voice,* she noted. The restraint around her ankle was checked and the footsteps retreated. She heard the scratching sound the door made as it was pulled closed. The chain was placed through the hasp and the padlock secured— only then did she move.

The food was in a Styrofoam container—the kind that could be bought over the counter at any grocery store deli. She didn't open it. The water was more of a temptation. She knew she was becoming dehydrated, but there had to be some kind of drug in it, otherwise she wouldn't have slept so long.

She sat deep in thought. *She had been drugged and brought to this place, when? It had been morning when she awakened. She had drunk the drugged cup of water and slept for at least ten hours. At some point the kidnapper returned to check on her. The water in the cup told her that. And now he had brought food and more water. What did he want with her?* She pushed the thought away. *No, I can't think of that right now.* The chain around her ankle was fastened to an iron stanchion. She tugged at it but it stood firm—no escape that way.

The wet jeans had repulsed him—what if she pretended to be ill? She lay back and closed her eyes.

She was huddled on a corner of the stained mattress when she heard the sound of a key in the padlock. That was her cue to lie down and moan. Before he came, she had exercised in her limited arc of movement until she was scarlet with exertion and sweat dripped off her. She rubbed the ankle shackle up and down her leg until it was red and sore. Pinching her cheeks had the same effect on her face. She threw off the blanket and moaned louder, her legs twitching and body jerking.

He dropped whatever he was carrying and rushed over to the mattress. Rough hands pulled her up and she felt the light of a flashlight on her face.

He let it fall and back-handed her, "Wake up, damn you, wake up."

She didn't respond and he dropped her back on the mattress. She heard him pacing up and down the length of the hut. His foot must have come in contact with the food container. He kicked it away with a string of curses. There was the sound of footsteps coming towards her mattress. She braced herself. The shackle dropped from her leg and she was dragged across the rough, concrete floor to the door.

The night air was cool and sweet. She briefly flirted with the idea of making a run for it. Before she could decide, he had the trunk of his car open and the opportunity was lost.

He dropped her into it, the lid slammed shut and the car bumped down a rough track before turning onto a smooth feeling road. The only way to judge distance was by time elapsed and she counted off the seconds. Four minutes from the hut to the road. A left turn and about twenty minutes on the smooth tarmac by her calculation, then a right turn and another five minutes of driving on a rough track before the car stopped and the engine turned off.

The trunk opened and she let her body go limp. She was dead weight and it was a struggle for him to pull her out. He dropped her on the ground then turned away, doubled over, trying to catch his breath. This was her chance and she seized it.

She darted to her feet, pushed him to the ground and started to run. She was in the middle of a corn field. The ears were brown and dry, almost ready to be harvested. It was impossible to move silently and the cracking and snapping of the tall stalks left a trail he could easily follow as she broke through. Behind her, she could hear him curse as he tripped in the darkness.

The edges of the sky were lightening. Dawn would soon break. She had no idea where she was headed, the corn was too high to see over, but she could hear him behind her. He had stopped yelling and was methodically following her. The ache in her legs was unbearable and her energy almost depleted. Suddenly the corn was gone and she was on some sort of open trail. Instead of following it towards the distant lights, she instinctively doubled back in the opposite direction, stumbling over the rough ground. Her feet went out from under her and she landed in shallow water. It was an irrigation ditch. She floundered forward until she saw an undercut in the bank. It was an opening she could crawl into. She squeezed in and collapsed.

Chapter 1

I scowled at the book I was supposed to be reading. American constitutional history was boring. I'd wanted the class on ancient Greeks or failing that, colonizing Romans. I would even have taken the medieval Brits with their endless wars and plagues, but they were all full. Students in the know signed up for them as soon as they became available. I was a novice freshman, which is why I was stuck with an adjunct professor who was as dull as his subject. To make matters worse, the class was a two-hour evening course. His monotonous voice droned on and on. At this rate, I would be catatonic before break came.

Mercifully, the droning voice finally stopped, "Break time. Be back in fifteen minutes."

There was a stampede toward the door and the clattering of feet down the stairs. I glanced down at my notes. They were totally incomprehensible. I would get more out of the class if I stayed home with my feet up on the couch, a glass of wine to hand and read the textbook by myself. I looked up. Too late, the teacher was heading my way and the last thing I wanted was another boring conversation with my incredibly boring teacher.

"Mrs. Conley, or, may I call you Kate?"

I moved closer to the door. "Gotta get coffee." Actually, I did. Usually, I'm a tea person, but I needed something to keep me awake until the end of class and tea out of a machine just doesn't work for me. He quickly moved in front of me, "Kate, I feel you're having a problem with chapters 6 and 7. Why don't we go for a drink later and discuss them?"

He flashed, what I'm sure he considered to be a winning smile, but it was actually just plain creepy.

"I'm sorry but I'm meeting a friend after class."

He gave me another smile which was almost a leer, "How about tomorrow? Say lunch? We could meet closer to where you live."

"I said I'm sorry. I can't meet you for coffee or lunch." My voice was a little sharper this time. I slipped around him and headed down the crowded stairs to the cafeteria.

Though the downtown campus of IUPUI served students of all ages, I was the only "non-traditional" in the class—a kind way of saying older than the rest—and therefore the only one close to his age group. But how many ways are there to signal someone that you're just not interested? According to my friend Sylvia, who was a lot more experienced at dating than I was—hundreds—and I was sure I'd used almost all of them. What was left? A tee shirt saying *I Am Definitely Not Available?*

By now most of the students were headed back upstairs, armed with filled coffee cups, and I was unquestionably swimming against the tide. A blond girl with an armful of books, careened into the side of me, throwing me off balance. At the same time, I felt a hand in the center of my back, and a definite push that sent me tumbling down the stairs with bodies scattering right and left. I landed on one foot, which bent under the pressure and gave way as I slowly slid to the cold, terrazzo floor.

I lay there dazed as the thundering feet faded into the distance.

"Are you all right, Mrs. Conley?"

I looked up to see an anxious face gazing down at me. It was Vincent, one of my fellow students.

"I think so."

I struggled to my feet and my right leg buckled under me. I collapsed back onto the stairs, "Maybe not. My ankle hurts—I think I've sprained it or something."

It felt more than a sprain—it hurt—a lot.

"Kate, what happened?"

And there was our sainted teacher, Ted, as he wanted us to call him, looming over me.

I started to say, "I fell…" but before I could get the words out, he interrupted.

"That leg doesn't look good. You need to go to the emergency room. I'll take you as soon as I finish class."

I shot a desperate glance at Vincent and he caught on right away, "I can take Mrs. Conley. Wishard Hospital's only a block away. I don't think we should wait. The ankle could be broken. I'll run upstairs and get our books." And without waiting for an answer, he took the steps two at a time.

Ted didn't look happy, "So you'll be over at Wishard? Don't worry, Kate. I'll come and get you as soon as I can."

Vincent came clattering down the stairs carrying my backpack, along with his, and Teacher Ted straightened up. "You take care of yourself and I'll see you soon." With a sour look at Vincent, he went back to class.

I breathed a sigh of relief, "I'm sorry to put you in the middle of this, but I really don't want that guy taking me anywhere. If you don't mind missing the rest of class could you drive me to my local ER and I'll make sure someone drives you back?"

He sat down next to me on the stairs and rested his thin arms on the knees of his threadbare jeans, "I don't mind, Mrs. Conley. I can get class notes from one of the other students. I was falling asleep anyway."

Despite his slight build, Vincent half-carried me to the door of Cavanaugh Hall and propped me up against a pillar. He ran across the street to my car which, fortunately, was parked in the first lot.

Even though Vincent was younger than my daughter Ellie, I considered him to be a friend—my only friend––at IUPUI, the Indianapolis campus of Indiana and Purdue Universities. In a class of eighteen-year-old freshmen, a woman fast approaching fifty stuck out like a sore thumb. But being the right age didn't seem to help Vincent fit in with his peers. He was as much of a misfit as I seemed to be. It could have been because he, like me, was never satisfied with any grade less than an *A* while too many of our classmates did the minimum required to just pass the course. It seemed natural we should study together when exam time came around.

The car pulled up next to the building and, with Vincent's help, I hobbled over to it and we started off towards my home town of Shelbyville which was about a twenty mile drive from Indianapolis.

Chapter 2

Vincent was a careful driver, a little too careful. He drove slowly, hunched over the steering wheel with a look of complete concentration on his face.

I thought I'd better ask, "Vincent, you do have a driver's license, don't you?"

He shot me a quick glance before riveting his eyes back to the road, "Yes, I passed the driving test but I don't have a car, so I'm out of practice."

I heaved a sigh of relief, tried to ease my throbbing ankle into a more comfortable position, then wished I hadn't when a stabbing pain shot up my leg. Before too long we pulled in under the portico of Major Hospital's emergency room.

My ankle was broken and I ended up with a big cast on my leg and an even bigger bill, that I hoped my insurance company would pay. It took forever: the x-rays, waiting for the results, then the doctor to read the x-rays, then someone else to put on the cast, then the first doctor again to prescribe pain medication and the do's and don'ts—mostly don'ts—of how to take care of a broken ankle. Finally, I was dumped into a wheelchair and taken back to an anxious Vincent.

He was relieved to see me. "Mrs. Conley, I hope you don't mind but I thought I should call someone to tell them where you were. I don't have a cell phone so I used yours and found the number of a Doris." He appeared slightly embarrassed. "Doris gave me directions to your house. She also asked if I were hungry."

I saw the bewildered look on his face and laughed. "That just means she'll have dinner waiting for us."

Doris was my landlady. After my divorce, which I won't go into because I was trying to forget all the years wasted on a useless, faithless man, I'd sold my home of twenty-five years and moved into an apartment in a beautiful old Victorian house in the heart of downtown Shelbyville, in Shelby County, Indiana.

Vincent pulled the car into the garage off the alley and with his help, plus my new crutches, I managed to make my way across the yard to our back door. Vincent opened it, but before I could maneuver my way through, Doris was there.

Her eyes were huge behind her thick glasses and her tight little gray curls were standing on end, "Kate, whatever happened? Vincent said you fell down some stairs at school and broke your ankle."

"That's about it, Doris." I didn't want to say anything about the hand in the middle of my back. I was still trying to decide whether or not it was accidental.

Doris yelled up the stairs, "She's here."

My artist neighbors, Rose and Enid came clattering down from their third floor apartment, followed by my dog, Digger, who pretty much has the run of the house. Normally Digger jumps all over me when I get home, covering my face with doggie kisses. But it was almost as if he knew he had to be gentle, so he restricted himself to a few soft whines and licks.

Enid and Rose helped me into the dining room, sat me down at the table and carefully propped my leg up on a spare chair.

"You sit over here, my little love." Doris found a place for Vincent. She bustled into the kitchen only to re-appear with ham, macaroni and cheese, green beans, a bowl of salad and a plate of hot biscuits. Vincent gazed in awe at the feast while Doris heaped his plate high and slid it in front of him. "Eat up, honey, there's cherry pie and ice-cream for dessert."

She turned to me. "Sam's coming over to eat but he doesn't know when."

That was typical. Sam is a detective with the Shelbyville Police Department and his hours depend on how much crime occurs on any particular day. He's also my boyfriend, significant other or, as the kids in my class would say, my BFF. In any event, we've been dating for almost a year and, yes, it was serious.

I heard the back door open and Sam walked into the dining room, "Sorry I'm late..." He broke off and stared at me. "Kate, what happened to your leg?"

His gaze went from the cast on my leg to my face, his amazing blue eyes filled with concern. I have to say that Sam is a very handsome man—tall, buff, with silver hair cropped short in an almost military cut. My heart skips all kinds of beats whenever he comes into a room. I should also say that he's a tad protective which I attribute to his job. He does, after all, see the seamy underside of Shelbyville society. I try to be understanding, but it gets a little annoying sometimes.

"Slipped and fell down the stairs at school. I broke my ankle." I waved across the table. "This is Vincent. He's in my American History class and he volunteered to drive me to the hospital."

Vincent looked up and nodded. Doris had just re-filled his plate and his mouth was full. She had also cut into the cherry pie and a big wedge, covered in ice-cream was in a bowl next to him.

Sam quickly helped himself and for the next few minutes conversation was muted as he and Vincent attended to the serious business of eating.

"Sam, Vincent needs a ride back to Indianapolis. Can you take him?"

Sam looked over at Vincent and laughed, "If you think we can wake him up."

Vincent was leaning against the back of his chair with mouth open and head hanging down. He was fast asleep.

Doris immediately took control. "Look at that poor boy. He's exhausted. Sam, let's put him in my spare bedroom and someone can run him back in the morning."

I could tell Sam wanted to protest but it was useless. If Doris decided Vincent was to stay, then stay he would. Within a few minutes, Vincent was firmly ensconced in Doris' guest bedroom and, according to Enid, fast asleep.

"I got him something to sleep in and I'm going to wash these so he'll have clean clothes to wear in the morning." Doris' hands were filled with Vincent's dirty laundry.

I was ready to sleep myself. It had been a stressful evening. Had someone really tried to push me down the stairs at school? No, it had to have been an accidental shove. Yet, I had definitely felt a hand in the middle of my back. I was too tired to think about it anymore. My crutches were next to my chair, but before I could reach for them Sam swept me up in his arms, carried me upstairs and into my bed where I promptly fell asleep.

Chapter 3

"Are you ready for your tea?"

Doris was busy hanging up my clothes from the night before. I vaguely remembered Sam swearing softly as he undressed me and put me to bed. Now I understood why. My jeans were mangled beyond repair. He must have cut them off me. Doris held out the sad looking remnants. "These are goners. I'll put them in the dust-rag pile." I heard the whistle of the tea kettle in the kitchen and Doris disappeared. She reappeared a few minutes later with a pot of tea with all the *accoutrements* and some toasted bagels.

"Sam left early but he said he'd drop Vincent back at his home in Indianapolis. I fixed them both breakfast before they left."

That was a given. Doris was barely five feet and an eighty-year-old human dynamo, who had the energy of someone half her age. She loved to cook and she loved to feed people. There was no way Sam or Vincent would escape without a full breakfast inside them.

"You know, that Vincent needs fattening up. He's way too thin."

I tried not to laugh. She'd said the same thing about Digger when I first got him. Her fattening technique was so successful that Digger was now restricted to diet dog food and an enhanced exercise regimen, which was the only thing that kept my weight in check because I ate far too many of Doris' dinners.

The phone rang. Doris got to it first. She listened for a moment, "Who did you say was calling? Dr. Ted

Thompson?" She looked over at me while I frantically signaled—*no*—and pantomimed sleeping.

"Mrs. Conley can't take any calls right now. She's still asleep." She gave me a thumbs-up sign. "No, I don't know when she'll be back to class. Yes, I'll be sure to give her the message." And she put down the phone.

"That was your history teacher. He wants to know if he can come by to give you class notes or something."

"Absolutely not, the guy is a total creep. If he turns up at the front door don't let him in."

Doris poured the tea and propped me up on my pillows. I could tell she was building up to asking me something. Sure enough, it was about Vincent.

"Kate, do you know anything about Vincent's family?"

"No, we've never talked about them. I'm only in one class with him and we study together for tests."

"Hmmm…" She moved a small table closer to the bed, made sure everything was within reach and said, "Call me when you need help. Vincent said the doctor told him you have to keep that leg propped up."

She paused on her way out the door. "You know you'll have to miss your next class. Maybe Vincent could come over and give you his notes. Somebody here could give him a ride."

Doris was shrewd and a lot smarter than people gave her credit for. I had noticed the night before that she seemed to bond with Vincent and I have to admit there was something sad and lonely about him. Doris had a big heart and it was obvious Vincent was going to be another of her strays.

Sam stopped by at lunch time to check on me and help me from the bed to the couch. "Sorry about cutting up your jeans, but it was the only way I could get them off you without hurting your ankle."

"You're usually more skilled at undressing me than that, so you're forgiven."

He grinned and slid his arm around my waist.

I leaned into him. "Did Vincent get home all right?"

Sam didn't say anything. He was too busy lifting me onto the couch and placing cushions behind my back. When he had my injured leg propped up to his satisfaction, he stood back and answered me.

"How well do you know him?"

"I've taken one class with him for half a semester and we study together for tests."

Sam was watching my face intently. He had his interrogation face on. "So, not very well right? How come he was the one who drove you home last night? Why didn't you call me, or Rose and Enid?"

"Sam, I fell down the stairs during class break and Vincent was the one who helped me. You were working and Rose and Enid were in Fountain Square setting up Rose's art exhibit. My teacher wanted me to wait until class was over and offered to take me to Wishard Hospital. I don't particularly like him so I accepted Vincent's offer of help and asked him to bring me to Shelbyville and Major Hospital." I sighed. "I would have called you but by the time you could have driven to IUPUI and then back to Shelbyville—it was much quicker the way we did it."

"Why don't you like your teacher?"

Trust Sam to focus on that.

"Because he keeps asking me to have coffee with him and I think he's creepy. Any other man could tell I'm not interested but he's oblivious."

"Why don't you tell him you're in a serious relationship?"

"Because he hasn't asked and it didn't seem an appropriate response."

"But it's appropriate to give control of your car to a virtual stranger."

I took a deep breath. "Sam, what's your problem with Vincent?"

"Doris asked me to take him back to Indianapolis this morning."

"And that was a problem?"

"No, but he had me drop him off at a block of apartments near campus. He said that was where he lived. I saw him go into the lobby but as I drove away, he came back out the door and went down the street."

"What's wrong with that?"

"Nothing, but it didn't look right somehow. I checked with the building manager and he doesn't live there and never has. So why did he lie to me?"

I couldn't answer him but I trusted Vincent. My instincts told me he was a good person. He must have had a reason for the deception. And that, in essence, was my one problem with Sam. He tried too hard to "protect" me and I didn't need protecting.

Recently he had what my landlady Doris would call, a flea in his ear. The flea was Sam wanting us to move in together. The moving in part was fine. Where he wanted us to live wasn't. I should explain that I'm a woman rapidly approaching her middle years, who, after being dumped by her sleaze-bag of a husband for a twenty-five year old blond bimbo, decided to go back to school and double major in anthropology and history. Sam was fine with the schooling and the fact that our time together would be limited due to his demanding job and my school schedule. His solution was that I should move into his apartment. I felt he should move into mine. So Sam and I were at an impasse!

I live in a beautifully restored Queen Anne house in a part of town that my ex-husband considers "bad" but I prefer to call "emerging". The house is divided into three apartments. Doris has the first floor, I have the second and our artist friends Rose and Enid have the top floor which includes attic space where they both have room for a studio.

I love my apartment. I love the high ceilings, the elaborate plaster medallions, the gleaming oak floors and beautiful stained glass. Sam's objection was that it would be like living in an "over-age sorority house" as he so eloquently phrased it. His apartment was in a modern block and had about as much character as a shipping container.

I tried to avoid the topic of moving altogether but Sam was a detective; he knew what I was doing. Whenever I changed the subject, a pulse in his clenched jaw would start to throb—a sure sign he was stressed. We would have to have the discussion one of these days, but I planned on putting it off as long as possible.

Today I used my distracting technique. "I don't know how I'm going to take a shower with this cast on my leg."

It worked. Sam came up behind me and enfolded me in his arms as he softly whispered, "I'd be happy to help solve that problem."

Chapter 4

By the second day of my enforced isolation, I was
bored out of my skull. Usually, I took classes three days
a week and volunteered at our local library the other
two, with weekends off. Now I was stuck on the living
room couch with my leg propped up on pillows. Doris
had left for the Senior Center where she was working
on a group quilt. She had placed my text books where I
could reach them.

"I'll be back in a couple of hours. Now don't you try
to get up off of that couch. You mustn't put any weight
on your leg and you know you can't manage those
crutches yet."

Enid and Rose had already left for Fountain Square,
a trendy neighborhood on the south side of
Indianapolis, known for its restaurants and artists
studios. Rose's exhibit would be opening in less than a
week. Sam was working a new case which seemed to
be taking up all his time. My daughter Ellie, also taking
classes at IUPUI, was at school and my four-year-old
twin grandsons, Johnny and Charlie, were with my
friend Frank, rather than me.

I was attempting to study but not getting very far. It
was too quiet. Usually the house was filled with people.
As well as Ellie and the boys, friends from the lovely
old Carnegie library, where I volunteered, frequently
stopped by, and Doris, Rose and Enid probably spent as
much time in my apartment as I did. But today Doris
was at her quilting circle. Rose and Enid would be in
Indianapolis for most of the day. Sam was too tied up at

the station to visit, even for a few minutes, and I was utterly alone.

The doctor at the emergency room had told me to keep the leg elevated and not put any weight on the injured ankle. I was still getting used to my crutches which meant I was pretty well confined to the couch.

I picked up my anthropology text book and started to read about the 19th century archaeologist, Heinrich Schliemann, discoverer of the lost city of Troy. Schliemann had actually visited Indianapolis in order to divorce his Russian wife so he could marry his very young Greek assistant. That was just a side-bar. I was supposed to be reading about the actual dig, methodology used, conclusions drawn, and the influence this had on later generations of archaeologists. But discovering that Indianapolis was once a mecca for men wanting to rid themselves of inconvenient wives—sort of like a Reno of the mid-west—fascinated me and I was wasting far too much time researching Schliemann's divorce.

My intercom buzzed. Doris had informed everyone who was likely to visit to stay away until she returned.

"Kate, I'm not having you get up and let people in when you're not supposed to walk on that leg. I'm only going to be gone a couple of hours. They can wait till I get home."

So I wasn't expecting anyone. Nevertheless, I struggled to heave myself up on one leg and prop my crutches under my arms. The caller was getting impatient. The buzzer rang again, a lot longer this time.

I paused. Using crutches was not easy and I was getting annoyed. When the buzzer rang for the third time, I said *to hell with you* and hobbled back to the couch. As I passed the window, I glanced down at the front path only to see my American History teacher, Ted Thompson, standing there, arms akimbo, staring up at my window. I hurriedly stepped back so he couldn't see me, and almost fell over.

He started towards the front porch again, seemed to think better of it, then moved toward the battered beige Camry parked by the front gate. The door slammed, there was a squeal of tires, and Ted drove away at high speed.

I found myself shaking with anger. How dare he come to my home uninvited? And what gave him the right to act out his rage on my front door buzzer. I sank back on the couch and picked up my book again.

It was no good. I couldn't concentrate on the written word. Sam was right. I needed to be blunt with the guy. He was personally repulsive and I didn't even like him as a teacher. Why did I always feel the need to be so damned polite?

I heard my kitchen door open. "Kate, it's me. I'm home." Doris came into the living room.

Almost at the same time the front doorbell rang. She rushed over to the intercom. "Come on up."

I heard pounding footsteps on the front stairs. Kevin, a young detective who worked with Sam and was engaged to Sam's daughter, Mira, put his head around the door.

"How's everything, Kate?"

"Boring. I'm tired of sitting here with my leg propped up. It's hard to get around on crutches. Daytime television is a joke and you're the only visitor I've had."

Kevin let out his infectious laugh, his round baby face aglow. "Sam would be here if he could but he's tied up with meetings all day. It's this new case he's working on. He asked me to stop by to make sure you're all right and check that you have everything you need."

Doris quickly answered, "You tell him not to worry none. Enid, Rose and me's taking good care of her. What's the new case?" Her faded eyes gleamed with curiosity.

His face flushed with dismay. Evidently he'd let something slip. "It's nothing, Doris—just the usual stuff."

He tried to change the subject, "You know Martha would come to see you too, but she's in the hospital for some surgery."

Martha was a patrol officer who also worked with Sam. We had met the previous year when Sam arrested me for chasing my cheating husband with a golf club. In my defense, I had caught said husband, *in flagrante delecto,* with his new personal assistant, on top of the antique desk I had bought him for his fiftieth birthday. I chose the first weapon that came to hand which happened to be one of Jack's golf clubs, which he had conveniently left by the office door, it supposedly being his golf afternoon. Since then, Martha and I had become close friends.

I was concerned. "Kevin, she didn't tell me she was having surgery. Is it something serious?"

Kevin blushed from his pink cheeks to his tow-colored hair and mumbled something about *a female thing* before telling me, "She's in Major Hospital. I think it'll take her a couple of weeks before she's back to work."

Doris interjected, "It's called a 'oofectomy' or something like that. It means she's having her ovaries removed."

Before Doris could go into details, Kevin hurriedly answered, "Yeah, that's it. Anyway, I was just checking on you for Sam. I've got to get back to the precinct."

The door slammed and I heard his footsteps clattering down the stairs.

"Doris, did you know about Martha's surgery?"

Of course she did; Doris knew everything.

"Why didn't you tell me?"

"You breaking your ankle put it clean out of my head."

I sighed. "Wish I could visit her."

Doris patted my shoulder. "We'll go tomorrow."

I looked at my propped up leg. "We?"

She beamed at me. "Sadie Simpson, down at the Senior Center, just went into a nursing home so I can borrow her wheelchair. It's a real fancy one. When Rose and Enid come home, we'll go pick it up."

Chapter 5

The next morning I was back on the couch waiting for Doris, Rose and Enid to take me to the hospital to visit Martha, when the front door bell rang. There was the murmur of voices, some excited squeals, the thundering of feet up the stairs and my twin grandsons raced into the living room.

"Grandma!" They ran toward me then abruptly stopped. "Can we draw pictures on your leg?"

"It won't hurt you." Charlie's green eyes, so like his grandfather Jack's, sought out mine. "Kayla broke her arm in kindergarten."

"Yeah," Johnny chimed in, "We got to write our names on her cast and draw hearts and everything but it didn't hurt."

"So can we draw on yours?" Their pleading eyes locked onto mine.

"Of course you can. You can draw anything you like on it."

"Thank you, grandma."

They gave me enthusiastic hugs and raced towards the door.

"Where are you going?"

"To get markers from Dodo." That was their name for Doris.

"And cookies, too." Johnny yelled back at me as they barreled down the stairs.

I laughed. Grandchildren were an unexpected joy.

There was the sound of someone clearing their throat. I looked up to see my son-in-law standing next to the window. I hadn't noticed him come in, "Andrew, what are you doing here?"

He looked embarrassed. "I thought I'd come over and check on you."

"You're not working today?"

"No, I took the day off."

"Aren't the boys supposed to be in school?"

He shrugged his shoulders. "It's closed—teacher's work day or something. I'm taking them to the Children's Museum in Indianapolis. They want to see the dinosaurs, but when they heard about your cast they got really excited and asked if we could stop in on the way so they could decorate it. That's all right, isn't it?"

"Of course it is. I always love to see them."

I suppose I should have added, "And you too," but we didn't have that kind of relationship. Andrew didn't like me and I didn't like him. He disapproved of my divorcing Ellie's father, of my going back to school, of my relationship with Sam and of my living in a house with two gay women. I was a little confused by this visit. Ellie was the one who usually brought the boys. Andrew and I saw each other only when we had to, such as family occasions. So why was he here?

"Kate, I wanted to ask you…"

"Yes…?"

He cleared his throat again, "What kind of classes are you taking?"

I was more than surprised. This was the first time Andrew had evinced the slightest interest in my schooling. "Right now I'm trying to get all my requirements out of the way, but I plan on double majoring in History and Anthropology."

"Why?"

"Because I love both subjects plus I quit college and have always regretted it."

He thought for a moment. "But you don't need to get a job so why do it?"

"It's not always about getting a job, Andrew. Isn't there something you would love to learn more about?"

"I have a family to support," he said stiffly. "I can't afford that luxury."

After graduation, I planned on going to grad school—maybe get an MLS and work as a librarian—or maybe not. There were many options and I planned on spending the next few years exploring them. I doubted Andrew could ever understand that sometimes you don't go to school just to train for a job. At this point I wasn't even sure about grad school. I might take classes in areas that interested me just for the love of learning.

"Well," he said defiantly, "I think it's really stupid that Ellie wants to take classes."

That was the moment Johnny and Charlie ran in through the door, their faces covered in cookie crumbs, followed by Doris carrying markers and a large plastic sheet.

"Let's put this on the couch then you can color your grandma's cast as much as you want."

The twins set to work with the markers and soon my cast was embellished with hearts and kisses plus strange looking animals that included a few ferocious dinosaurs. Andrew stayed remarkably quiet and left as soon as he could tear the twins away from their new art project.

With her porcelain complexion, long blond curls and air of fragility, Rose would seem to be the last person able to help me downstairs in a fireman's lift. But appearances can be deceptive and she was a lot stronger than she looked. Neither she nor the more sturdy, Enid, had any problem carrying me. Once we got to the hospital, Sadie Simpson's electric wheelchair was the perfect vehicle. It was so easy to tool around in, I wondered if there were some way I could use it at school to get to and from class.

Doris was happy to demonstrate all its functions, "Look, you can tilt it back or raise and lower the seat. If you want to sit, you can put up the foot thingie and it's just like a recliner." It was exactly as she had described it—a real fancy wheelchair.

Enid and Rose had dropped us at the hospital. They were finishing the final details on the exhibit and couldn't stay.

Doris brought homemade cookies and chocolates for Martha. "Enid and Rose wanted to bring a couple of bottles of that wine you like so well, but they didn't think the hospital would allow it, so it'll be waiting for you when you get out of here. When are you being discharged?"

"Either tomorrow or the next day—doctor's decision."

"Who's going to take care of you when you get home?"

"I'll be fine, Doris. I'm not like Kate. I can move around. I won't need any help."

I saw the set of Doris' lips. Like it or not, Martha was going to have help and Doris was going to be the helper.

"What's going on down at the station? Kate and me have barely seen Sam the last few days."

"I don't know. It must be something big. None of the guys have been by to see me, either." Martha's homely face reflected her disappointment.

"Hmm." Doris looked thoughtful. "I haven't heard anything. Has Sam said anything, Kate?"

"No, you know he doesn't talk about work very much."

Doris dropped the subject, but I could tell she was still thinking about it. Which meant that somehow she was going to find out what was going on and when she found out she would tell me.

Our library manager, Sebastian came through the door bearing a large bouquet of pink and white roses, "Martha, my love, how are you?"

Martha cheered up right away. Sebastian had that effect on almost everyone. He gave her a gentle hug. "Stephen sends his love, too. He's fully booked today, but he had a cancellation for tomorrow, so he'll stop by to see you then."

Stephen was Sebastian's partner and also my beautician. He had just opened his own shop in Shelbyville, and by all accounts, it was going to be a success.

Sylvia, our librarian, made an entrance preceded by a giant teddy bear that looked remarkably like Sebastian. She was, after all, the leading lady of our local community theater. Clarice, our self appointed, head volunteer at the library followed her. I had christened Sylvia, my dating guru because, after a failed thirty-year marriage, I needed dating advice and Sylvia dated more than anyone I knew. Recently she had found what she termed "the one" and it seemed her speed dating days were over. And since I had Sam, I didn't need any more advice anyway.

The last to arrive was solid dependable Frank, another library volunteer. He kissed Martha on the cheek and presented her with a bowl of fruit, some of it from his own garden. It was almost a mini reunion and we stayed until visiting hours were over and the nurse told us to leave.

"We'll see you tomorrow, Martha," Doris added, "Then we can talk about who's going to take care of you once you're home."

We all crowded into the elevator and rode down together. The doors opened at the ground floor. Sam was standing there. I was so surprised to see him I hit the wrong button on the hi-tech wheelchair and almost ran him down. He jumped out of the way and I hastily found the right control and stopped the chair before it went careening down the corridor.

He held onto the arm. "Kate, what are you doing here? Is anything wrong?"

"I'm fine. We were visiting Martha. Is that why you're here? She said nobody from the station had visited her yet."

Sam opened his mouth to reply. I heard someone give a discreet cough. A female officer that I didn't recognize was standing next to the elevator holding the door open.

"Yep, I'd better get up there," he quickly answered and hurriedly stepped inside. The doors closed behind him and I was left wondering why Sam couldn't have taken a few minutes to talk to me when we'd hardly seen each other the last couple of days, why the tips of his ears had turned red, and why the elevator went straight up to the fifth floor when Martha's room was on the third.

Chapter 6

"Why don't you call Vincent?" Doris asked as she was pouring my tea for the fourth time that day. "Maybe you could study together."

"He doesn't have a phone," I answered, "and I don't know where he lives."

"Well, Sam would know. He took him home the other morning."

I debated telling her that Vincent had lied to Sam about where he lived then decided she'd probably find out anyway.

"Sam said Vincent didn't live in the apartment building where he dropped him off. That he lied to him about living there."

Doris pursed her lips. "Maybe he just didn't want Sam to know. Some people are private that way."

I should have known Doris would defend him. ·

"Frank said he'd take me down to your school and I'm going to pick up all your class notes for you. Then you won't have that teacher you don't like coming around again."

"Doris, you don't have to do that. Ellie can pick them up after her class tomorrow."

"Well, Frank's already on his way over. It's all arranged."

I knew any argument I could make would be useless. When she'd brought my tea this morning, she'd had a head full of pink, plastic curlers. That meant she was going somewhere special. Her mission was not to get my class notes. Doris was determined to see Vincent.

The buzzer on the intercom sounded. Doris hurried over to the door. "That must be Frank now."

But it was my daughter, Ellie, and I knew as soon as she walked through the door that something serious had happened.

Doris saw it too. "I'll wait for Frank downstairs."

Ellie watched her leave. "Where's Doris off to?"

"Down to school, she's going to pick up my class notes for me."

"She doesn't have to do that. Your teachers can email them and I can pick up any hand-outs."

"Try telling that to Doris. She has her own agenda."

"Which is?"

I explained about Doris wanting to meet Vincent again and concluded with, "She took a liking to him and now she thinks he needs looking after."

"She's probably right, Mom. He wears the same two shirts and he's got duct tape holding one of his shoes together."

I hadn't noticed, but I bet Doris had.

Ellie stood in front of the couch. "Mom, I want to talk to you about something."

She looked tense.

"Sit down. What is it?"

Instead of sitting, Ellie wandered over to the gate-leg table near the window and started to rearrange the English cottages I collected. She looked distracted and I began to worry about their safety—they were fragile pieces and chipped easily. Finally, she turned back to me and I heaved a sigh of relief.

"It's Andrew. You know he's always been opposed to my going back to school, but lately it's getting worse. We do nothing but argue. I've tried talking to him, telling him how I feel, why I want to go to college but he just doesn't get it. He doesn't even hear me. He called my going to school a fad."

She walked back to the couch. "He's acting like some biblical patriarch and he thinks I'm as stupid as his mother."

Ellie was right about Andrew's mother. She was, if not totally stupid, then definitely on the fast track towards it. Anyone of a different ethnicity terrified her, as did people with tattoos, gay couples, non-churchgoers or anyone who looked or acted outside her limited view of what she considered to be the norm.

His father was no prize either. At Ellie and Andrew's wedding, her new father-in-law had cornered me behind a large floral arrangement and tried to lay a slobbering kiss on my lips. When he wouldn't let go of me, I had slapped his face, hard. I told Jack about the incident. To his credit, and I don't give him credit for much, Jack had taken him outside and threatened to punch him. He'd also told him if he ever laid one finger on Ellie, he would rip his head off.

"Mom, I don't want to live this way. I'm wondering if I want to stay married to him."

I was shocked. I knew they were having problems but had no idea it had reached the point of divorce. "Ellie, have you thought this through?"

She gave me what I always referred to as her mule face, the one I got when, two days after she graduated high school, she announced she was engaged to Andrew and wasn't going to college. I couldn't shake her resolve then and doubted if I could now.

"Yes, Mom. Of course, I've thought it through."

"Have you discussed it with Andrew?"

She paused. For the first time, I saw her resolve waver.

"Not yet. I wanted to talk to you first. You've been through a divorce. I need to know about the financial end of it. Would I be able to support the boys by myself?"

I took a deep breath. I had to tread carefully.

"Ellie, when I married your father we were both college students. I quit my classes and took a full time job to put him through law school. My money paid for most of his schooling and supported the office for the first year. I also worked without pay until you were born. After that, I filled in when our secretary went on vacation and still kept the books until business warranted hiring an accountant."

"And how did that affect the divorce?"

"It only affected the settlement. We split all the assets of the marriage down the middle and since I have an equal share in the business, your father still has to pay me half the profits."

Ellie sat down opposite me. "So what are you saying?"

"You won't get that. Are you prepared to work fulltime and raise two children on your own while trying to get an education? You've never held a job. It won't be easy, Ellie."

She was silent.

"Let me ask you this. Has Andrew been unfaithful to you?"

"No. Andrew would never do that." Ellie seemed shocked that I would even ask the question.

"So the big issue is your going to school. Why does he feel threatened by that?"

She sighed. "I don't know."

"Then you need to find out before you do something irrevocable."

"I guess."

I thought for a moment. "Ellie, you and Andrew haven't had any time away from the boys since they were born. What if you went away for a long weekend? I could take care of Johnny and Charlie." I looked down at my leg. "Well, with Doris and Frank's help. You could talk this through together. If it doesn't work maybe try couple's counseling. Up until now you've had a good marriage. Don't be in too much of a hurry to end it."

A plethora of emotions passed across her face. In the end she sighed. "Maybe you're right, Mom. I suppose I shouldn't give up so easily." She added, "But I refuse to be treated like a child who's too stupid to make its own decisions. Andrew is going to treat me as an adult."

She came over and gave me a hug. "Thanks for the advice. I'll let you know about the weekend away."

After Ellie left, my phone pinged. It was a text from Sam, *Can't make it tonight. Will call you when I can.*

Maybe I was the one in need of relationship advice!

Chapter 7

"Kate, let's go to lunch today."

Doris had come back from school yesterday with her hopes of finding Vincent completely dashed. "I got all your notes and handouts, but Vincent wasn't anywhere to be found," she'd told me.

"Why is seeing Vincent so important to you?"

"I have a feeling he needs help. I still have Charlie's money and I thought we could use that for a scholarship or something to get him through school."

Charlie was Doris' cousin, who had died the previous year. He left his not inconsiderable estate to Doris who had placed it into a charitable trust. I was one of the trustees.

"Doris, I'll be going back to my classes in a few days—I can contact Vincent for you."

She had brightened up right away and this morning was back to her usual, indefatigable self.

"Martha suggested we meet for lunch. Frank can help you downstairs. We'll take the wheelchair with us and it's a nice day, so we can sit outside on the restaurant's patio."

I was tired of studying and a little excursion sounded like fun. "Is Martha up for it? She's only been out of the hospital for a few days."

"When I was over at her place yesterday, she told me she was ready to go back to work, even if it's just desk duty for now."

"Where are we going?"

"It's a new place near the hospital. A lot of her co-workers hang out there. She says there's something big going on down at the station but nobody is talking about it."

"And she might meet someone who'll spill the beans, so to speak?"

Doris shrugged. "Don't you want to know why Sam has been MIA this past week?"

I did, but I was willing to wait until Sam was ready to tell me. There were reasons he kept things to himself, though I had to admit I was curious.

Frank picked us up and he supported my one-legged hop downstairs. We reached the restaurant in plenty of time to meet Martha. It was great to be somewhere other than my apartment and I think Martha felt the same sense of freedom, so we were all in a festive mood as I guided the wheelchair up the ramp and around the side of the building to the covered patio.

I abruptly stopped. My little band almost ran into the back of me. Sitting at a small corner table with an attractive, blond woman who was dressed in nurses' scrubs, was Sam. She had her hand on his arm and they were huddled, heads close together, engaged in an intense conversation. Sam looked up and, instead of being happy to see me, a look of utter dismay crossed his face.

He quickly came over and knelt next to my chair. "Kate, why are you here?"

Martha, Frank and Doris hurried off to a larger table in the opposite corner.

"I'm here for lunch with my friends. How about you?"

The tips of his ears were fast turning red. "It's…I…it's business Kate."

"Sam."

I looked over to his table. The woman was tapping her wristwatch. "I've got to get back."

"I'll be right there, Nora."

I let off the brake on the wheelchair. "Don't let me keep you from your business meeting."

Sam bent forward to kiss me but I turned my head and his lips barely grazed my cheek. He started to say something. I released the brake and the chair shot forward. He quickly moved out of the way and I maneuvered myself to the table and my waiting friends, keeping my back to Sam and his lunch date. There was a brief silence. Then I heard Sam's receding footsteps.

For a few moments no one said a word, then Doris asked, "Who was that woman with Sam?"

"That's Nora. She and Sam used to date…" Martha broke off, "that was before he met you, Kate. That was years ago. It was nothing serious. Sam ended it …"

Her square-jawed face flushed. "Really, she works at the hospital and they still run into each other occasionally." She finally realized she was making matters worse. "Why don't we order?"

It had been five days since I'd seen Sam. He'd called and texted me a few times—calls that were usually interrupted when Sam gave me a quick—*have to go*—and hung up. So he was too busy to spare a few minutes to stop by and see me, but not too busy to take an old girlfriend to lunch?

Doris handed me a menu. By then, I was no longer hungry.

My phone pinged with a text. *I'm outside. Can I come up?* It was Sam.

I texted back, *I'm already in bed.*

His answer was, *Please.*

Two minutes later I heard him at the back door. I set the book I was reading aside as he came into the bedroom. He looked exhausted, his face gray and drawn.

"Kate, I want to explain about today."

"No need, Sam. You can have lunch with any of your old girlfriends. You certainly don't need my permission."

He swore softly under his breath, "Kate, it was business. I needed information about a patient from Nora. She didn't feel comfortable speaking to me in the hospital in case we were overheard."

He sat down on the edge of the bed and tried to take my hand. I moved it away.

A pulse in his jaw started to throb. "I suppose Martha's told you that Nora and I once dated."

"She did. But that's okay, Sam. You were single a long time. I'm sure you dated a lot of women. I don't need a list."

"Kate, I know you're angry…"

I looked up at him. "I was hurt Sam, not angry. I accept that sometimes you get so involved in your work that everything else has to take a back seat. But I didn't expect you to find time for an ex-girlfriend and ignore me."

"Kate," he tried to take my hand again. His phone rang. He looked down at the display. "I have to take this."

He walked out into the hallway. I heard him say, "Nora, what is it?" There was silence then, "I'll be there as soon as I can."

He came back into the bedroom, "Kate, I have to go…"

But by then I had switched off my bedside lamp and turned away from him. He sighed and the next sound I heard was the closing of the kitchen door.

Chapter 8

Three days passed with no word from Sam. I decided I would return to school after the weekend was over. Cavanaugh Hall, the building in which I took all my classes was fully ADA accessible. If other students could navigate its halls in wheelchairs so could I. In any event, finals would be here in less than three weeks and I wanted to pass all my classes.

Doris put her head around my door. "You need any help getting ready, Kate?"

"No, I'm done."

I looked at myself in the mirror. I wore a long skirt with a black and gold top that was a favorite of mine. Stephen had styled my hair and I'd taken extra care with my make-up. I looked good tonight, I told myself, but what did it matter? The one person I wanted to impress wouldn't be there.

We were on our way to Rose's art exhibit in Fountain Square. Frank was driving and Margaret, the wardrobe mistress at our local community theater, with whom Frank was "keeping company" as he so quaintly phrased it, was sitting in the front, with Doris and me in the back of the car.

Doris and Margaret were catching up on all the theater gossip. I was idly glancing out of the window when I heard, "Well, she says she wants to help backstage but nobody likes her and she causes trouble wherever she goes."

Doris chimed in, "Her husband's left her for another woman. I think the divorce'll be final in a few weeks.

Sebastian's so soft-hearted he feels sorry for her and will probably let her join the company." She sighed, "It's not going to work—a leopard can't change its spots."

"I know," said Margaret. She sighed too.

"Who can't change what?"

Doris answered me, "Barbara Armstrong—you know the one you call the Bitch."

Doris and Margaret were right. Barbara Armstrong was the wife of my ex-husband's accountant and had been a bitch for the thirty years I had known her. She was the one who had announced my ex-husband's affair with his new and very young secretary in front of a museum board meeting at our local country club. She had loved my shocked reaction while pretending to commiserate with me. This past year, her vicious gossip had almost ruined my relationship with Sam. She was, without a doubt, the nastiest woman I had ever met. If she were in any way involved with our theater group, I wouldn't be.

"Is Sebastian really going to let her in?"

"He feels sorry for her—thinks she's becoming an alcoholic. She's always in the bar at Luigi's. Sebastian thinks he can save the world. But there are some people who'll never change and she's one of them."

Doris was right. Bitch Barbara's main goal in life seemed to be hurting other people. I was glad when we arrived at our destination and could talk about something else. To even hear her name angered me.

The exhibit space was a large converted warehouse. The brick walls were covered with Rose's paintings and the space in front of them filled with loud, chattering people. There were even more people lined up at the bar for the free wine that was usually served at these events.

"Look at them all. Rose should be pleased that she got such a big crowd. I'm going to give tours and help her sell them paintings."

Actually, I found Rose's art work disturbing. She herself was tiny and frail-looking, like a delicate, porcelain figurine in human form. Her paintings however, reflected a darker side. The canvases were filled with heavy swirls of vitriolic paint that illustrated a deep, dark rage. Her work had quite a following and was beginning to sell well.

"Doris, you go mingle. I'm going to park myself over here."

"Are you sure, Kate?"

"Positive."

Doris didn't need any coaxing; she loved mingling. "I'll be back in a few minutes to check on you."

I parked in an unobtrusive corner and took my time observing the crowded room.

"Kate Conley?"

I looked up to see a blond, burly middle-aged man standing over me.

Seeing my bewildered look, he said, "David, David Ashcroft. We were in high school together. I was on the wrestling team."

"You were captain."

What I didn't say was that, before I met Jack, we had briefly dated.

"Yes, I heard you were divorced.

"I am."

"Me too, maybe we could get together one of these days—catch up on old times."

There really were no old times to catch up on. I had dated him twice then dropped him when I saw his first wrestling meet. If I remembered correctly, it was because I hated how he looked in his, less than flattering, uniform.

I pointed to the cast on my leg, "I'm somewhat limited these days."

The back of my neck tingled. Turning my wheelchair slightly, I looked towards the door. To my amazement, Sam was standing in the doorway glaring at us. Martha was behind him. With a look of determination on his face, he strode over, knelt next to the wheelchair and tried to kiss me on the lips. I moved my head slightly and the kiss landed in the vicinity of my right ear. Undeterred, he stood up, arm still around my shoulders and put out his hand to David, "Sam Williamson."

David shook his hand and hurriedly left. I saw Martha turn away to hide a grin.

I looked up at Sam. "You wouldn't be marking your territory would you?"

He tightened his arm around me, "Is it still mine to mark?"

"Do you want it to be?"

"Kate, you know...."

"Kate."

Mira, Sam's daughter, was hurrying towards me. As usual, she looked beautiful, her auburn curls spilling over one shoulder. She had Sam's vivid blue eyes. Kevin, her fiancé was right behind her. Since Mira lived and worked in Cincinnati, which was over an hour away from Shelbyville, their time together was limited and Kevin rarely moved from her side when she was in town. I wondered if they had finalized their wedding plans. The last time Mira and I had discussed it, she and her mother were arguing about almost everything.

She hugged me. "How's the leg, Kate? When does the cast come off?"

"A few more weeks..."

I saw Kevin whisper in Sam's ear. They both looked towards the door. The woman from the restaurant was standing there scanning the room.

Sam cursed softly. "How in the hell did she find out about Rose's exhibit?"

Kevin hung his head. "Sorry, that was my fault. I ran into her at the hospital. We got to talking and she asked me what I was doing this weekend. I told her Mira would be in town and we were coming here. She said it sounded interesting but I swear Sam, I didn't invite her."

Sam looked down at me. "You want to mark *your* territory?"

I smiled, "Do I need to, Sam?"

He answered me by dropping a kiss on my head and walked over to her. "Nora, what are you doing here? I didn't know you were into art?"

She flushed. "I've never been to an exhibit. I thought I'd see what it's all about."

"I know someone who can help you."

He waved Doris over. "Doris, this is Nora. She's a nurse at Major Hospital and she needs someone to give her a tour of the exhibit."

I stopped him. "Introduce me, Sam."

Sam looked a little unsure but he went ahead. "Kate, this is Nora Jenkins. She's been helping me with a case I'm working on."

I held out my hand. "Hi, I'm Kate Conley. I saw you at the restaurant the other day but we didn't have time to talk."

She looked slightly embarrassed. "I was on my lunch hour and had to get back to work."

Doris interjected, "Which one of Sam's cases are you helping with?"

Nora looked questioningly at Sam. He shook his head. "Nora can't talk about it, Doris, so stick to art tonight."

"You come with me, honey." A disappointed Doris whisked Nora away. "Now this is from her blue period..." Her voice trailed away. Martha followed her.

Kevin looked at Sam's face and took Mira's arm. "We'd better go with them. Doris can be very persuasive."

Sam sat down in the chair next to me and took my hand, "Kate, let me explain about Nora..."

I shook my head. "You don't have to Sam. I know you're in the middle of something important—I was missing you and feeling sorry for myself. Though," I added, "it would be nice to get a call or text from you once in a while."

He sighed. "I wasn't sure what to say. You seemed pretty angry and I tend to say the wrong thing and make matters worse. That's why I came here tonight to talk to you in person and tell you I'm sorry."

He looked at me, his amazing blue eyes pleading with me.

I covered his hand with mine. "I'm sorry too, Sam."

He kissed me again, on the lips this time. It was a very satisfying kiss.

"I'm going to get us a glass of wine."

He walked towards the bar. I noticed more than a few heads turn to watch him, not all of them women. I also noticed that Sam was totally unaware of the attention he created. And when he came back, his focus was on me only.

As he handed me the glass his eyes searched my face, "Are we all right, Kate?"

I smiled. "We're getting there, Sam."

He raised his glass, "To us."

We took one sip and almost choked.

"Kate, want to go somewhere where the wine is drinkable and we can talk?"

I was about to suggest my apartment when Sam's phone buzzed. He groaned. There was a muttered conversation, and a terse, "I'll be there." Sam turned back to me. "Kate…"

Across the room, I saw Martha check her phone. She nodded at Sam and made her way to the door. I pulled him down to my level. "You have to leave, right?"

"I'm sorry, it can't wait."

He looked so dejected I laughed. "Go save the world, Sam. We'll get together when we can."

"Kate, you're okay with this?"

"Disappointed, but okay."

His face lit up. We shared a lingering kiss and though I didn't see him for the rest of the weekend, his calls and texting almost made up for it.

Chapter 9

Navigating around school in my borrowed wheelchair was a lot harder than I anticipated. With elevators, plus automatic doors, I could get in and out of the classrooms but once inside, steering around chairs and desks was difficult and, too often, I found myself trapped by book bags left carelessly in the middle of aisles or chairs pulled out from tables. Except for Vincent, the students in my classes rarely noticed when I needed help and I was forced to ask, which I hated. Since I was also unable to drive, Fred, Enid and Rose took turns chauffeuring me to and from school.

My first two classes were fine. The teachers barely noticed me with the wheelchair. But they were large classes and they'd barely noticed me *without* the wheelchair. The problems arose with Wednesday night history.

At first Dr. Ted was thrilled to see me back in class. He made a big fuss about moving desks to accommodate my wheelchair then called on me an excessive number of times to answer questions. Even though I tried not to make eye contact he seemed to be watching me constantly. Sam was right. I needed to set this guy straight.

At break time I waited until the other students had left the room. He came over to my desk and stood next to me.

I backed up the wheelchair a little. "Can you not stand so close to me? It makes me uncomfortable."

He gave me his creepy smile. "Well, Kate, I've missed you. What if we go for a cup of coffee or better yet some wine and catch up on everything?"

I gritted my teeth. "There's nothing to catch up on. I have all the class notes I need."

He moved even closer. "I meant catch up on us."

I took a deep breath. "There is no 'us', Dr. Thompson. You are simply one of my teachers. I don't want to see you, meet you, or have coffee or wine with you, and as for your coming uninvited to my house, don't you think that borders on harassment?"

His face turned so red I thought he was going to explode. "You...you flatter yourself, Mrs. Conley. What makes you think I'm interested in you? I was simply trying to help a student. I have a roomful of beautiful, young girls..."

"Who are surrounded by handsome, muscular young men. What's your point?"

He started to splutter, 'I...I...' then fell silent.

"So can I assume the unwanted attentions are going to cease and I won't have to report you to the administration?"

He put his face so close to mine, I could feel his hot breath on my cheek. "Don't you dare threaten me..."

He broke off as students started to stream back into the room.

Vincent's worried face told me that he picked up on the tense atmosphere. The rest of the evening didn't get any better. There were no more questions and instead of creepy smiles, I got looks of sheer malevolence whenever Teacher Ted's eyes caught mine.

After class, as I waited for the elevator, he came up behind me. "How lucky that we have an elevator to accommodate your wheelchair. Going downstairs on crutches could be quite dangerous; someone could easily push you off balance."

The elevator stopped at our floor. He smirked at me. "Are you coming?"

I shook my head. "No, I'll wait for the next one."

The door closed and he disappeared from view. I was stunned. Did Dr. Ted Thompson just threaten me, or did he confess to pushing me downstairs the night I broke my ankle? Why would he do that? I thought back to that evening. He had invited me to meet him after class for coffee and I had turned him down. It couldn't be for something that trivial. But I had the uncomfortable feeling that it could. The end of the semester seemed a long way away.

Chapter 10

Due to the almost terminal boredom of staying home alone, I was back to my volunteer job at the library. Since it was only two blocks from the house, I didn't need a chauffeur. I was able to use the wheelchair. Frank had helped me down the stairs and walked alongside me though, as I told him, I was pretty sure I could manage on my own.

Doris had argued vehemently, "Of course you'll need Frank's help. What if you get caught on a curb or something?"

I tried to tell her that the street was accessible all the way to the ramp at the library side entrance but she wouldn't hear of it. "Frank's taking you and that's that." She was probably right. I was still learning how to open doors and not get the wheelchair stuck in them.

Clarice and Sylvia greeted me with hugs, but I didn't see Sebastian anywhere.

"Is he in today?"

They looked at each other. There was an awkward silence then Sylvia answered, "I think he had an appointment. He'll be here by lunchtime."

Bossy Clarice pushed me toward the workroom. "You can't shelve books from your wheelchair so I thought you could do some of the check in and process patron holds."

I was halfway through my second box of returns when Sebastian came up behind me. "Kate, I'm sorry I wasn't here to greet you, but I had an appointment at the theater."

He was beaming and I knew he had good news to impart. "Did you hear the theater board has decided to let me direct *The Heiress*?"

I hadn't but I was thrilled for him. Since he was fairly new to directing, he was usually given the plays that nobody else wanted. This time *The Heiress* was his first choice and it would be a new experience for him.

"Kate, you will audition won't you? Doris said you'll be out of the wheelchair in a couple of weeks and by opening night you should be totally healed. We open in mid-January so it shouldn't conflict with your school schedule."

I'd had a part in Sebastian's first production for our local community theater. It was a terrible play, a florid melodrama written by a founding member of the group, but he had turned it into a farcical comedy which was a big hit and probably the reason he had moved up in the directing hierarchy.

"So you'll be there next Thursday?"

"No, I think I'll have to give auditions a pass this time around."

He looked completely taken aback. "But why? The role of *Elizabeth Almond* is perfect for you and even if you're still in a walking cast the costume will hide it."

Instead of answering him, I asked my own question, "Sebastian, I've heard that Barbara Armstrong is going to join the company. Is that true?"

"Yes, she wants to work backstage and we always need volunteers."

"That's the reason."

He sighed. "I know you and Barbara have had your differences but, poor woman, her husband has just left her after over thirty years of marriage. I think you of all people could relate to that. Have some empathy for her."

Did Sebastian really ask me to have empathy for someone who appeared to be saccharine sweet but in reality was a venomous snake?

"If you knew what I know about Barbara Armstrong...."

Sebastian stopped me. "Barbara's told me that you resent her because she was the one who divulged your husband's affair with his secretary. She was only trying to help and she's devastated that you misunderstood her motive. I can't believe you could be so petty."

I snapped back, "And I can't believe you could be so stupid. The woman's a monster and no way will I spend any time around her. By the way, it's ex-husband and she was his personal assistant, not a secretary."

With that I signed out of the computer, grabbed my purse, swung the wheelchair around and headed for the exit. Clarice and Sylvia tried to stop me, but I steered around them, out the staff entrance and down the ramp.

Before I was halfway home I realized that there would be nobody at the house to help me up to my apartment. No way was I going back to the library to ask for help. Doris had a saying for everything. The appropriate one for today was, "where there's a will, there's a way." I'd make it up the stairs even if I had to crawl. Negotiating the back gate wasn't easy, but I managed to steer up to the porch, pull myself out of the seat and inch slowly inside the door. The flight of stairs up to my apartment back door looked steep but I took a deep breath, sat on the bottom step, pushed off with my good leg and struggled to the top, one laborious stair at a time.

I dug the door keys out of my purse and glanced up at the lock. Damn! I couldn't reach it. It was too high. I looked around for something to hold onto so I could drag myself upright. There was nothing. Doris, Enid and Rose weren't home. I didn't want to contact Sam.

The only option available was to call Frank or someone else from the library. That meant Sebastian would learn about it. No way was I doing that. I pounded on the door in frustration. There was a soft yip and a bewildered Digger scrambled through his dog flap and started barking. The door opened and I looked up into Sam's startled eyes.

"Kate, what on earth..." He knelt down, gently lifted me up, carried me into the living room and deposited me on the couch. An anxious Digger followed behind.

"Clarice called and told me you'd left the library by yourself. I came over to make sure you got home safely, but you weren't here. I was on my way to look for you when Digger barked."

He was frowning. "I thought Frank was going to escort you home and help you upstairs."

"I was in a hurry, Sam. I didn't tell him I was leaving."

"How did you get up the stairs to the kitchen door?"

"I sat on the bottom step and pushed off with my good leg."

I saw his face. "Sam, I was careful. I took it one step at a time."

"What if I hadn't been here to open the door? What if you fell?"

"But you were and I didn't."

He shook his head in frustration. "Kate, tell me what happened at work to make you so angry?"

"Why do you think I'm angry...?" I sighed. "All right, Sebastian asked me to audition for the play he'll be directing at the theater."

"It couldn't have been that."

"No." I pulled him down next to me on the couch. "Doris and Margaret told me Barbara Armstrong will be joining the company and working backstage. I told Sebastian if she were there then I wouldn't be."

"Understandable."

"He said I should have empathy for her. He also called me petty."

Sam put his arms around me and drew me close. "I'm sorry, Kate. Sebastian doesn't know the part that woman played in what happened last summer. I could talk to him…"

"No! If he prefers to take her word over mine, so be it."

He chuckled. "You know that look that Ellie gets when she's certain she's right—the one you call her mule face? Now I know where she gets it."

I pushed him away. "If you think this is funny you can just leave."

His phone rang. He checked the display and sighed, "What is it, Kevin?" He listened a moment longer, "Give me an hour and I'll be there. No, one hour. They can wait thirty minutes longer."

Evidently that wasn't acceptable. I heard more muttered conversation then he came back to the couch. "I'm sorry, Kate I have to go." He took my hands in his. "Please be patient. I swear I'll make this up to you."

He looked so miserable I threw my arms around his neck and kissed him. He kissed me back. We made up so thoroughly that by the time he left, he was whistling a tune as he went down the stairs.

Chapter 11

This was my last history class before finals. Just one more week! I knew it was going to be unpleasant as I wheeled myself through the door. The desks had been re-arranged again. This time I couldn't navigate my wheelchair through them. I parked myself in a corner and, with the help of two other students, found an open desk where I could place my books and notebook.

Even though I tried to avoid him, I caught my teacher's eye. He gave me a triumphant smirk and I knew he was the one who had done the re-arranging. The petty little man also refused to call on me and lavished extravagant praise on those who did answer his questions, as if to show me how out of favor I was.

By the time everyone went downstairs for coffee I'd had enough. Even though Frank wouldn't be picking me up for another hour, I decided to study alone in the break room until he arrived. When I heard the students coming up the stairs, I wheeled myself out of the room and took the elevator to the basement.

The cafeteria was empty except for someone at a table in the far corner. I navigated over to the coffee machine but decided to get hot chocolate instead. It was slightly less disgusting than the coffee. As I put the cup on the table next to my backpack, I saw that the "someone" in the corner was one of the students in my class. She had her head down on the table sleeping, with her blond hair almost covering her face. It was a common enough sight, lots of students took a power nap in between classes, but I decided to check on her anyway.

I made my way over to the table and shook her shoulder gently but she didn't awaken. Her color was fine and she was breathing regularly so I decided to let her sleep. She would probably be awake by the time I was ready to leave. I navigated my way back to my table and took a sip of hot chocolate. It was coffee! I must have pushed the wrong button on the machine. I took a few more sips...

I awoke in a dark, confined space. My head was lying on something hard and metallic. Whatever it was dug into the side of my face and there was a cloying smell of disinfectant in my nostrils.

As I sat up my head started to swim and I felt the nausea rising. I took deep breaths until it subsided and looked around. In the dim light that seeped in around the door, I could see brooms and mops hanging on the wall. Next to me was a bucket and in the opposite corner a large trash can. It was the janitor's closet in the basement. *How and why was I here?*

I tried to piece my scattered thoughts together. I had been in class. Then I went down to the cafeteria to study and decided to stay until Frank picked me up. There had been something after that, but I couldn't remember what, then nothing. *No, I had smelled something in the closet, not just the pine disinfectant, but what had it been?* No matter how hard I tried I couldn't remember. It was as if someone had taken a giant eraser and wiped my brain clean.

I looked around for my phone. I had left it in my backpack but my backpack wasn't with me. I remembered having it but where was it now? I painfully hauled myself to my feet, trying not to put any weight on my injured ankle, and tested the door. It was locked.

So someone had to have put me in the closet. But who? And why?

In the distance I heard footsteps. I would have yelled for help but some instinct stopped me. The sound came closer then stopped outside the door. There was fumbling then the sound of a key in the lock. I hung onto the doorknob for stability trying to keep upright. As soon as I felt it start to turn, I pushed the door open as hard as I could. It slammed back against the wall, taking whoever had opened the door with it.

"Damn it."

I recognized the voice. It was my creepy, history teacher. He was holding onto his head as he leaned against the wall, almost trapped behind the heavy door. I didn't want to injure my ankle any further but I had no choice. Hobbling down the hallway I held onto the walls for balance.

He straightened up and started to come after me, "Stop, get back here."

I got as far as the corner and almost ran into my wheelchair. He was still yelling, "Come back here!"

My crutches were lying across the seat. I picked one up and threw it towards him. He staggered backwards and I was able to push the wheelchair at him. It zigzagged down the corridor and he got tangled up in the wheels. The chair fell over taking him with it. He landed heavily, still shouting at me.

As I stumbled down the hallway, I passed an open door. A hand came out and grabbed my arm. Before I could scream another hand covered my mouth. A familiar voice whispered in my ear, "Mrs. Conley it's me, Vincent."

He pulled me through the door, closed it quietly and put his arm around my waist, supporting my weight, "We can hide in here."

The room was pitch black. I couldn't see a thing, "Where are we?"

"It's the boiler room. I sleep in here sometimes."

We stopped. The door from the hallway opened and lights came on. Ted Thompson came into the room then halted. I could hear his heavy breathing. Vincent froze and squeezed my arm warningly. After a few more seconds, the lights went out and the door closed. Further down the corridor we could hear more doors opening and closing.

I felt Vincent relax and he pulled me around a corner where we shuffled towards a far wall. Just when I thought we were trapped I saw another opening and a gap behind some large machinery, "In here," Vincent breathed, "he'll never find you."

He pulled me into the small space. There was an old sleeping bag on the floor. My backpack and Vincent's were next to it.

He whispered, "I found your bag in the break room on one of the tables. You'd left the classroom at least an hour before. I looked and couldn't find you anywhere so I used your phone to call Detective Williamson to see if you'd arrived home. He was on his way here because Frank…"

The door crashed open, the lights came on again and I heard footsteps. Vincent grabbed my cell phone. He mouthed, "I'm going to tell the detective where we are and who's looking for us." His fingers raced over the keyboard. The footsteps came closer. We stood rigid. I heaved a silent sigh of relief when they moved away.

Our stalker started to sound agitated. "Kate, come out now, or you'll be sorry when I find you."

I could hear him panting as he moved around the open space. He started banging on the machinery in frustration. His voice rose until he was almost screaming, "I know you're in here somewhere!"

My phone pinged. We both grabbed for it but Vincent got there first. He snatched it away from me and turned it off. We froze, barely breathing, but he'd heard it. It was in the taunting tone of his voice, "I'm coming to get you, Mrs. Conley."

He came closer. "Better come out now."

Vincent grabbed my hand and squeezed it tightly. He pushed me further back in the space and stood in front of me. The footsteps were almost to us when the door slammed open. Our stalker turned and ran. There was the sound of thundering footsteps, a scuffle, a cry of pain, and an agonized scream as multiple bodies slammed into him.

I heard Sam's voice over the din, "Kate, Vincent!"

Vincent yelled, "We're over here!"

Sam came sprinting around the corner and gathered me up in his arms. He was breathing heavily and I could feel the thudding of his heart against mine. He held me away from him and looked intently at my face. "Did he hurt you?"

I shook my head. "No, he never got near us."

Vincent stood back shyly. Sam put his arm around him in a brief hug. Then, with an embarrassed, "Thanks Vincent," he quickly released him and turned to me, still out of breath, "When Frank came to pick you up and you weren't here, he called Rose and Enid, and then me. I was on my way when Vincent texted me and told me exactly where you were."

Two detectives came around the corner. I recognized them from the station but couldn't remember their names, "We're taking him down to lock-up." I could hear yelling and screaming in the distance. Ted Thompson was not going quietly. There was a muffled curse and a cry of pain, then nothing. Teacher Ted had finally been silenced. The older of the two men touched

Sam gently on the shoulder. "Hey, bud, we'll take it from here. Are you all right, ma'am?"

Before I could answer him, Sam's phone pinged. He handed me over and moved away to take the call.

I knew by the agonized look on his face what he was going to say, "I'm sorry, Kate. I have to go. Martha's here. She'll take care of you. The EMT's are on their way. I'll catch up with you at the hospital."

As he left, I heard him say, "Full blood tests right away…"

The older detective stopped him, "We know the routine, Sam. We'll get the leg checked out, too." Sam reached the corner then turned back and spoke to both detectives, "Hey, Kreutz, Hanley, will you make sure Vincent gets back to Kate's house tonight?"

"Sam, I told you—we got this."

With another anxious look at me, Sam finally left.

It was late when we finished up at the hospital. After blood tests, which showed faint traces of the date rape drug Rohypnol, and x-rays of my leg which luckily incurred no further damage, Vincent and I were briefly questioned, though I wasn't much help. I could remember being in class. I vaguely remembered being in the break room and then I woke up in the janitor's closet. I knew there was more but it just wouldn't come and I ended up feeling totally frustrated and useless. Martha drove us back to the house where Doris, Rose and Enid were anxiously waiting up for us.

Doris' face was bright pink with agitation and her gray curls were standing up in little peaks. "Frank just left. He was going to the hospital to check on you. I'd better call him and tell him you're home."

Enid and Rose helped me up the stairs and into bed while Doris took Vincent into her apartment. I was exhausted but couldn't fall asleep. I tossed and turned until at some point in the night I came out of a restless slumber and saw Sam slumped in a chair, silhouetted against the light that came in from the street light outside the bedroom window.

I propped myself up on one elbow. "Sam, come to bed."

He looked over at me. "It wasn't him, Kate."

It took a moment to register. "Not him? You mean Ted Thompson wasn't the one who locked me in the closet? But he knew I was there. He chased me. He was screaming my name."

"I have no doubt, Kate, that he's involved in this. Kreutz said he was smirking during the whole interview as if he was getting away with something, as if he knew they wouldn't be able to prove anything. In the end, they had to let him go."

I was bewildered. "He practically admitted he was the one who pushed me down the stairs."

Sam moved quickly over to the bed. He took me by the shoulders and turned me towards him. "What do you mean, pushed you down the stairs? When you broke your ankle? You told me it was a fall."

"I didn't say anything because I wasn't sure. It wasn't until he threatened me..."

"Why haven't you told me this before?" Sam's voice was low and tense.

"Sam, that night the stairs were crowded. I was going down, but most of the students were coming up, going back to class. A girl bumped into the side of me and that's when I felt the hand in the middle of my back."

Before he could say anything else I tried to explain, "It could have been an accident—just someone off balance—I didn't think it was necessary to worry you over something that was probably nothing."

"Who was close to you?"

"Vincent was the one who helped me, but Ted Thompson was there almost at the same time. He wanted to take me to the emergency room as soon as he finished the class. That's why I asked Vincent to bring me to Major Hospital."

"What reason would Thompson have to push you? Did you have any kind of confrontation?"

"He asked me to have coffee with him after class and I said no. I wasn't very polite about it."

Sam ran a hand over his face. "Tell me about the threat. What were his exact words?"

"At break we were both waiting for the elevator. He said something about how lucky I was that I didn't have to walk down the stairs on crutches because I could have another accident."

"That was it?"

My head was throbbing. "I don't know, Sam. I can't remember any more, just that I felt threatened."

He gently eased me back on my pillows and covered me with the quilt. "It's all right. We'll talk in the morning when you're more rested."

Later, I felt him creep into bed. He put an arm around me. I nestled into him and fell asleep.

Chapter 12

When I awoke, Sam's side of the bed was empty. There was the sound of raised voices coming from the kitchen. The deep timbre of Sam's voice was recognizable but the others were barely audible.

I hurriedly threw on some clothes and as I limped down the hallway, I heard Sam thunder out, "No, absolutely not! You will not get involved in this in any way."

I hobbled through the kitchen door and there was immediate silence. Doris sat at the table with lips clamped firmly together, arms folded across her chest. Vincent sat next to her. He looked distressed. A red-faced, angry Sam loomed over them. He saw me and with two quick strides hurried to my side, gathered me up in his arms, and helped me into a chair next to Doris.

"Kate, what happened to your cast?" Doris was definitely agitated, her hair looked worse than it had last night and, instead of her usual housedress and apron she was wearing her old, flannel robe and slippers.

"When they x-rayed my leg in the emergency room they said the cast could come off. All I need now is this boot thing and I'll be through with all of it in two or three weeks."

I looked around. "Why all the yelling?"

Doris gave one of her snorts. "You tell her, Sam."

He shot her an angry look then turned to me. "Kate, I told you last night Ted Thompson wasn't the one who drugged and locked you in the closet."

"Yes," I answered, unsure of what was going on.

"Kreutz and Hanley, the two detectives who interrogated him last night, are certain he's involved. The thing is, he didn't leave the classroom after you went downstairs. He stayed until the last student was gone. When they questioned him about why he went to the basement, he said it was because he uses the exit there. It's the one closest to the parking garage. We checked and it is."

"But he knew I was in the closet."

"His explanation is that as he was passing he heard a noise and unlocked the door to see what it was. He was angry because you slammed the door into his face and opened a cut on his head. Hell, his lawyer was even talking about pressing assault charges against you."

"Why did he chase me? What about the screaming and the threats?"

"He said you and Vincent had no business being in the boiler room and, as a teacher, it was his job to check on his students."

"So he wasn't involved...?"

"We're sure he was involved." Sam's tone was grim. "Someone drugged you and put you in that closet. Ted Thompson..." He broke off and took a moment to pull himself together. "We think he was going to take the next step."

"Which was?"

Sam turned away and shook his head.

Doris had been quiet long enough. She piped up. "She'll never go for it, Sam, and we've already got it covered."

"Will someone please tell me what *it* is? And what you have covered?"

Before he could stop her, Doris blurted out, "Sam thinks you shouldn't go back to school until this is all sorted out, but I told him you wouldn't go for that."

Give up a whole semester of work? Doris was right. I only had three finals then school would be over until the end of January.

Sam sat down opposite me. He took my hand and I could feel the tension in his body. "Kate, I know you don't want to miss final exams, but this guy is dangerous, and right now we have no idea who he's working with. I think your safety is more important than any grade you might receive."

I shook my head. "I won't miss finals, Sam."

He got up from the table and turned away from me. For a moment I thought he was going to punch the wall. Instead, he leaned over the kitchen counter, breathing heavily.

Doris started to say something but Sam put his hand up to stop her. "This can't be repeated."

He walked over to us, his laser eyes boring into ours, until all three of us nodded acquiescence.

"What I couldn't tell you, Kate, is this. Three weeks ago we got a call from a farmer out in the county. He was harvesting his corn and found a young girl half in and half out of an irrigation ditch. She was in pretty bad shape. We didn't have any missing person reports, she had no identification and, judging by her condition, she had been in the ditch for a few days. It was a miracle she survived at all. From the abrasions on her right leg, we figured she had been chained up somewhere. She was put in ICU at Major Hospital and Nora was one of the nurses assigned to her."

Sam sat down next to me again. "That's why I had to meet daily with Nora. She and the other nurses were taking notes on everything this girl said as she drifted in and out of consciousness. Her doctors wouldn't let us question her until she was out of ICU so we were stymied."

"You know, Sam, if you'd explained..."

"I hated keeping things from you, but I couldn't, Kate." He got up and moved slowly around the room. "We kept it out of the newspapers because we didn't want the perpetrator to know she'd been found. In the course of our investigation, we found that over the last seven years, three other girls from IUPUI have gone missing. She was in your history class…"

His jaw clamped tight and he turned away from me. "I needed to get this cleared up as fast as possible."

"Do you still think Ted Thompson is involved?"

"We can't prove anything yet, but yes, I'm sure he's involved." He hesitated for a moment then went on, "Kate, are you sure you won't consider …"

"No, Sam. I'm not throwing away a whole semester of work."

He started to speak but I stopped him, "I will be careful. I promise." I showed him my leg. "Look, my big, heavy cast is off. My ankle is almost healed and I only have to wear this boot thing. No more wheelchair."

"Why won't you listen, just this once?"

"I'm not letting some creepy little man dictate what I do."

Doris had sat silent long enough. "Sam, I told you, we got this covered."

Before she could get any further, Sam stopped her, "Doris, this isn't a case for amateurs. What I just told you is strictly confidential. You will not, I repeat NOT get involved in this case in any way." His tone of voice softened when he saw the hurt look on her face. "I can't do my job if I have to worry about a bunch of slaphappy, wannabe detectives getting in the way. The police department will handle this."

Doris wasn't going to give up without a fight. She started ticking off points on her fingers. "But, Sam, there's Frank, Enid, Rose, and me. That teacher has never met any of us. Frank and me know where all the rooms are. We went there to get Kate's class notes when she warn't able to go to school. There's people of all ages taking classes at IUPUI." She gave one of her sniffs. "Old people are invisible."

She went on in a more gentle tone of voice, "Sam, we're only going to watch out for Kate. We don't want anything bad to happen to her."

He ran his hand over his face. "Doris, I don't want anything to happen to you, either."

"Nothing will happen to any of us. We'll sit outside the exam room and pretend to be studying. Then we'll follow Kate everywhere she goes. We're going to watch out for Ellie, too. If we need more people, I can get them from the Senior Center. They'd love to do it."

Sam shook his head. "I don't need any help. I mean it. If I find any one of you interfering in a police investigation, I will have you arrested."

Doris stood. "Come on, Vincent. We're wasting our time here."

And she left, slamming the door behind her.

Sam sighed. "Kate, I'll have someone at IUPUI watching out for you."

"Is that necessary, Sam? Vincent has finals the same days that I do. He'll be driving me."

"About that, why doesn't Frank drive you? Then Vincent can stay in Indianapolis instead of at Doris' apartment."

"What's your problem with Vincent?"

Sam was walking towards the back door. He turned to me. "Kate, who was first on the scene when you fell and broke your ankle?"

"Vincent, then Dr. Thompson." I stopped. "Surely, Sam, you can't suspect Vincent? He was the one who saved me when I was locked in the closet."

"But he was first on the scene that night, again with Ted Thompson, coincidence or something more?"

He left through the kitchen door and I was left to wonder.

Chapter 13

I was thankful that Frank was driving me to the library this morning. Though I was ambulatory, I had been cautioned against walking too much and I wouldn't be allowed to drive until the boot came off.

It was good to be rid of the wheelchair, though I would be forever grateful to Sadie Simpson for her generous loan. But for her, I would still be confined to the house and dependent on friends for transportation. Now I could walk short distances and no longer had to hop around my apartment or have someone carry me up and down the stairs.

I was nervous about encountering Sebastian. We had not left on good terms and as soon as Frank and I entered the building, I knew that had not changed. Sebastian saw me as I came in the door, but when I moved towards him he lowered his eyes and disappeared into the break room.

Sylvia was behind the librarian's desk. "Hi, Kate, how's the leg doing? Frank says you're in a walking cast now." But it wasn't the usual enthusiastic greeting she gave everyone and I wondered if she was mad at me, too.

I was saved by Clarice. She hurried over to me. "It's lovely to see you out of that heavy cast, but Doris says you still have to stay off the leg as much as possible. You can sit at the computer in the work room and check in returns. Come on."

She bustled away and I trailed after her. As soon as we were alone, she turned to me and whispered, "I'm glad you're back. It's miserable around here. Sebastian's cranky all the time, Sylvia's not herself—I don't know what's wrong—but it's all that woman's fault."

"What woman?"

"Oh, Kate, you know who I'm talking about—Bitch Barbara."

I was shocked. I didn't know Clarice was aware I called her that.

"Don't be embarrassed. I've known her all my life and that's the perfect name for her. We were in the same class all through school. She was Nellie Wiedermeyer then, and the most nasty, spiteful, mean-spirited girl I ever met." Clarice pulled her cardigan around her thin shoulders and tightened her lips. "I don't know how she got her hooks into Sebastian, but it's started already."

"What's started?"

Clarice pulled a chair over next to me. She sat with her head close to mine. Anyone entering the room would have taken us for a couple of conspirators. "To start with, you and Sebastian used to be best friends. Now you're at loggerheads."

I wasn't sure what loggerheads were but they didn't sound good, so I nodded anyway.

"Stephen says he doesn't have time to do hair and make-up for the play." She sat back nodding her head, "You know how he loves working with Sebastian. Why would he say that? And did you notice how distant Sylvia was?"

Clarice moved closer and hissed in my ear, "That's all happened since that woman joined the theater group."

"Clarice, that's really sad. Sebastian was thrilled for the chance to direct *The Heiress*. It sounds as if it's going to be a disaster."

"No. It won't," she said firmly. "I'm joining the theater group and I'll report back to everyone. I won't let Nasty Nellie Wiedermeyer ruin it for him. That woman has no interest in theater whatsoever, so what's her agenda? I want to know. You mark my words, I'm going to find out."

One of our volunteers came in dragging another cart of returned books.

"Hi, Kate. I hear the ankle is improving."

I smiled back at her. "Every day!"

She sat down at a table in front of a large pile of periodicals ready to be checked in and picked up the top magazine. There was going to be no more sharing confidential information.

Clarice winked at me, "We'll talk more, later."

Chapter 14

I had my feet up on the couch and a glass of wine to hand, studying for my biology final. Digger was stretched out at my feet. He raised his head, gave a short yip then raced towards the kitchen to greet Sam.

Sam almost dragged himself into the living room. He looked utterly drained. "I'm sorry about this morning. I was out of line. I don't mean to imply that you can't make your own decisions…"

"Sam, it's all right. We argue but we always get over it."

"Then you're not mad at me?"

I kissed him gently on the cheek. "I'm not mad at you."

He held me close then reluctantly let me go, "Kate, this morning I didn't tell you everything. The girl we found was a student in your history class. One day, she simply didn't turn up. Nobody thought that unusual. Dr. Thompson has a lousy reputation as a teacher and half the original class had already dropped out. When we talked to some of the other students, they told us that he and this particular girl had heated arguments in class and he seemed angry with her. We didn't discover who she was until a few days ago. She lived at home with her parents, not on campus. They were on a cruise in the Caribbean, but didn't know she was missing until they got back to find the mail box stuffed with letters and newspapers piled up on the porch. They immediately contacted the university, found she hadn't turned up for any of her classes then called the police."

"I've spent a lot of time with her and her parents. At first she remembered very little of what happened. It's almost a carbon copy of what you told us. She'd had a big argument with Dr. Ted and left the class. She went into the break room, got a cup of coffee from the machine and woke up in an outbuilding with a chain around her leg."

"Do you think she'll remember anything more?"

"That's kind of hazy right now. As her health improves, so does her memory. I'm hopeful she can give us more information when she fully recovers."

"What happened to the other students who went missing?"

"There were three of them. The first was found in Brown County wandering around the countryside, dazed and confused. She'd been missing for almost two weeks and had no idea where she was or how she got there. Two years later, another girl disappeared. This one was found near Bloomington when she staggered out of a wooded area close to the highway. It was the weekend of NCAA basketball finals at IU and was dismissed as some kind of prank. The girls were found in different parts of the state, two years apart, so nobody connected the abductions. They'd been held captive, but the place where they were kept was never found. They all had lesions around their ankles, but apart from that they seemed unharmed, that is they hadn't been..."

The tips of his ears turned red and he coughed. "You know..."

I took pity on him and didn't enquire further. "And the third?"

"Her body was found in some woods east of here. It was early winter and there was a freak snowstorm. She died of hypothermia. All three were found in different counties, which is why nobody connected them at first.

This girl was found in Shelby County and when we checked for similar crimes we realized that all of these women had gone missing while taking classes at IUPUI."

"And the motive?"

"At this point, we don't know."

"Sam, I do remember one thing. It wasn't hot chocolate."

"What wasn't?"

"What I drank that night. The coffee in the machine is so bad that I got hot chocolate instead, but it turned out to be coffee, which is why I didn't finish it."

"And why you didn't sleep that long. The cup you left on the table was over half full."

His phone rang. He answered with a curt, "Williamson."

I saw his face change and knew he was going to leave.

He looked up from his phone, "Kate, another girl is missing."

Chapter 15

My phone pinged. It was a text.

'*are yOustil uP*'.

I read it again but it still didn't make sense. It pinged once more, '*thi Is mynew pone*'.

One more time, '*doRis*'.

I sent back my answer, 'Come on up.'

Doris came into the apartment bearing a smart phone in her hand and a big grin on her face. "Did you get my texts?"

"Doris, when did you get a cell phone?"

"Today. Almost everyone at the Senior Center has one, but I never needed anything like that till now. I asked Vincent where I could get one and him and me went to the phone store. I got one for each of us." She shrugged her thin shoulders. "It was a special deal—two for one or something. Now he's teaching me how to use it. I'm a fast learner. I know how to text already."

Maybe spelling and punctuation would be next on the list.

"Why do you need a cell phone *now*?"

Doris paused; for a moment she was speechless. "Well...most people at the Center's got one. I thought I'd see what they're all about."

But she couldn't look me in the eye. I started to ask more questions, but she quickly changed the subject.

"Kate, I want to talk to you about Vincent."

She stopped, lost in thought, twisting her apron string around her finger. Looking up, she said, "Do you know he's never had a family? He's been in foster care all his life. When they reach the age of eighteen, they're on their own. That's why he's sleeping in the boiler room at IUPUI and doing odd jobs to pay his way through school."

That explained a lot about Vincent. "How long has he been in foster care?"

"He thinks all his life—at least as long as he remembers. I've been thinking…" Her mind went off on another tangent. I waited her out.

"He's a real good person and I want to give him money from Charlie's fund. What do you call it—a stipend. I think he gets some government money to pay for his school, but not enough that he can afford a decent place to live or a car or phone or new clothes. He wouldn't tell me much just that sleeping in the boiler room is better than a homeless shelter."

She was silent for a moment then, "I want him to live with me. I have a spare room or better yet, what do you think about converting half the basement into an apartment for him or even the loft over the garage? He's kind of private so maybe that would be better for him."

"That's a big step, Doris. You hardly know him. What does Vincent think about it?"

She shook her head. "I haven't said anything yet. I asked him to stay until your leg is all healed up and you were able to drive again. He's real independent. He wasn't going to take the phone until I told him we needed it for our protection detail."

"Your what?"

The dismayed look on Doris' face told me she had let something slip. She tried to cover, but it was too late. "Kate, that's just for fun. It's what we call it down at the Senior Center. Chuck and Frannie Oppenheim wanted to name it, Underground Ops, but they were voted down."

I could understand why Sam didn't want amateurs getting involved in a police investigation. "Doris, Sam asked you to keep what he told you about the investigation confidential. This isn't a game. The people doing this are dangerous. We don't want anyone getting hurt and the fewer involved the better."

"Kate, I haven't said anything about what Sam told us. I only mentioned that I might need some help following somebody and I couldn't tell them who. It was on a strictly 'need to know basis'. Don't worry, Kate. We're not going to interfere in anything."

"So you're telling me that you'll stay away from school and leave everything to Sam, right?"

"I won't be going to IUPUI."

"And the others?"

She gave one of her sniffs. "I'm not responsible for what other people do."

That wasn't the answer I wanted.

Chapter 16

I was remembering things. I had tossed and turned the previous night partly because I was having strange dreams, but mostly because I was missing Sam and the bed felt lonely and empty. When I awoke, I couldn't remember what the dreams were and it wasn't until I was sitting in the kitchen, drinking my second cup of tea, that fragments started floating through my brain.

Dr. Ted and the smirk he had on his face that night, as if he knew something I didn't. Blonde hair, the smell of perfume—no, not perfume—something else. Something about the closet—but what?

I called Detective Kreutz. His phone was busy so I tried Hanley's and got an answer. "Hi, this is Kate Conley. You asked me to call if I started to remember anything."

"That night is coming back to you?"

"Yes, first of all—"

He interrupted, "No, let's do this face to face. Are you at home?"

I told him I was.

"We'll be there in about fifteen minutes." He added, "That's all right with you, ma'am, isn't it?"

I'd barely put the coffee on when the front door bell rang. I buzzed them in and opened the door to my apartment.

They entered bringing with them that peculiarly masculine odor, a blend of stale cigarette smoke, the cold air of outdoors and a faint hint of testosterone. I wondered which of them was the smoker. My guess was Kreutz. He had that slightly wrinkled drawn, look long term smokers seem to acquire. There was an air of excitement about them.

I brought in the coffee. Hanley set up a tape recorder. "You don't mind do you, ma'am? It's easier than relying solely on notes."

I shook my head and took a deep breath. "Last night I had a hard time sleeping. My dreams kept me awake and this morning I started to remember what they were."

Hanley interrupted me, "Let's start with what you remember about that whole day. The night we talked to you, you weren't exactly coherent. We'll take it step by step. That particular day, you were still in a wheelchair, correct?"

I nodded then remembered to say yes for the tape recorder.

"Who drove you to school?"

"A friend of ours, Frank."

"Ours?"

"My landlady Doris, Rose and Enid..."

He interrupted again, "Full names please."

"Doris Weppler, Rose Clancy and Enid Waterman— they share the top apartment and Doris lives on the first floor. Frank is Frank Busse. We both volunteer at the Shelby County Library. Rose, Enid and Frank take turns driving me to and from class. Well, now Vincent is staying with Doris, he drives me also," I paused. "I don't know Vincent's last name."

Hanley interjected, "We got it, ma'am. So that day it was Frank's turn?"

"Yes, he dropped me off and wheeled me to the elevator, then told me he'd be back at nine to pick me up."

Detective Hanley continued with the questions while Kreutz sat silent, occasionally taking notes.

"Tell me about class."

"When I got to class, the desks had been re-arranged and it was difficult to steer my wheelchair around them. I finally managed to squeeze into a corner. After the break, I decided to go down to the cafeteria in the basement and study alone."

Detective Kreutz interjected, "Was there a reason for that?"

"Dr. Ted Thompson is a poor teacher and I get more out of reading the textbook alone than I do in his class. Also…"

"Also, what?"

He leaned forward on the couch looking keenly at my face.

"Dr. Ted, as he likes us to call him, was smirking at me all through class. I know he was the one who moved the desks just to make it difficult for me and he wanted me to know it."

"Why would he do that?" That was Detective Kreutz again.

This was a little embarrassing. "Ever since I started the class he's been too attentive to me. He always calls on me to answer questions and praises me extravagantly when I'm correct. He keeps inviting me to go for coffee or a drink after class. Sam said…"

I saw a look pass between them. Detective Hanley turned away to hide a grin.

"Anyway, he invited me again and I decided to bring to an end any delusions he might have about a relationship with me."

"You said what?"

"That I didn't ever want to have coffee or wine with him and, if he came to my house again, I would report him to the administration for harassment."

Detective Hanley jumped in, "I hadn't heard he came to your house."

"I didn't answer the door so he went away."

Detective Kreutz took over the questioning, "Was that the end of it?"

"There was one more thing. The night I broke my ankle, he had asked me out for a drink. I told him no and he suggested lunch the next day. I turned him down again, not very politely. When I went downstairs at the break, it was crowded with students coming up. A student almost fell into me and at the same time, I felt a definite push which sent me flying down the stairs, but I wasn't sure if it was accidental or not. The night I told him I would report him if he bothered me again, I ran into him by the elevator and he said something about how lucky there were elevators to accommodate my wheelchair because I could have a nasty accident if I went down the stairs on my crutches. Someone could push me."

"So you think he was threatening you."

"I'm not sure, but it felt like it. He was smirking again as if he knew something I didn't."

"The day of the incident when you were locked in the janitor's closet, you went down to the cafeteria where you took your class breaks?"

"Yes, it closes in the evening but there's a machine where you can get coffee and hot chocolate. The coffee is really bad, so I decided to get hot chocolate instead. I remember going into the room in my wheelchair. I put my backpack on the table, got out the coins and wheeled myself to the machine. As I came back to my table, I saw a young girl in the corner, sleeping."

I broke off. "No, I noticed her when I first came into the cafeteria. I thought she was taking a nap—a lot of students do—anyway, I put my hot chocolate on the table and went over to check on her."

"Can you give us a description?"

I rubbed my eyes. This is where it got shaky.

Detective Kreutz turned off the recorder. "Hey, Phil, I think Mrs. Conley could do with a cup of tea." He grinned at me. "Sam said that's your beverage of choice. He'd be here if he weren't scouring the countryside looking for a kidnapped girl."

I must have let my surprise show because he went on, "It's okay, it's confidential, but you have to share some things. It's not easy being in a relationship when you're a law enforcement officer."

Detective Phil came back with my tea and I drank almost half the mug before he turned the tape recorder back on and I continued, "The girl was blonde. She had her head down on the table with her hair hiding her face. I still recognized her as one of the students in my class, though I didn't know her name."

I drank some more tea. "I shook her shoulder but she didn't stir. She was in a deep sleep. I decided she was taking a nap and resolved to check on her again before I left."

"Then…?"

"Then I went back to the table. I remember drinking from the paper cup, but it was coffee not hot chocolate. I thought I must have pressed the wrong button on the machine but I drank it anyway."

Kreutz shook his head. "You didn't drink much. There was three quarters of the cup left which is probably why you didn't sleep that long."

"Anything else you remember?"

"The smell."

He looked at me. The other detective leaned closer.

"I noticed it when I bent over the girl at the table. It wasn't a perfume that I recognized. I think it was more like a shampoo—it smelled something like coconut. When I was in the janitor's closet, I thought I got a hint of the same fragrance."

"Are you saying she was in there with you?"

"She wasn't there when I woke up. But…I'm sorry, I'm just not sure, I think at some point I smelled it."

"You said last night that you heard someone walking along the corridor, but you didn't call out to them. Why?"

"The footsteps didn't sound right. I can't explain it but I felt…" I searched for the right word, "threatened. I had pulled myself up and was hanging onto the door knob. As the door started to open, I pushed it as hard as I could and ran—well, hobbled."

I closed my eyes and buried my head in my hands as I relived those panic stricken moments.

Detective Kreutz stood. "We'll leave the rest until tomorrow."

I sat up in my chair, "Can we finish it now?"

"Are you sure you're up for it?"

"Yes. There's not a lot more to tell. The door hit Dr. Thompson's head and it took him a few moments to recover." I took a deep breath then went on, "He came after me, but as I turned the corner, I almost ran into my wheelchair. My crutches were lying across the seat. I picked one up and threw it at him. He tripped over it and I pushed the chair towards him. He got tangled up in it and fell. That's when Vincent grabbed me by the arm and pulled me into the boiler room. He steered me towards where he…"

I stopped. I didn't want to get Vincent in trouble.

"It's all right, Mrs. Conley, Vincent told us that he sometimes sleeps down there."

"He had my backpack with my phone and he texted Sam, Detective Williamson. Then Ted Thompson came in and turned on the lights. He was screaming and banging on the machinery. I don't think he knew Vincent was in there because he only called out my name. A text came in on my phone and he heard it. Then you all came in and you know the rest."

I leaned back in my chair. I was exhausted.

Detective Kreutz patted my shoulder again. "Thank you, you've answered a lot of questions we had. We'll probably have more but that's enough for now."

Chapter 17

My phone pinged. Another text.

'*cOMe donw Now*'

There was only one person who could have sent it so I texted back '*OK*'.

When I walked into Doris' living room, Rose, Enid, Frank and Margaret were already sitting on the couch.

Doris led us into the kitchen. "Clarice will be back soon. She had to go home to let her dog out. We're having a meeting about Sebastian."

Evidently, it had been going on for some time. The table was littered with empty coffee cups and the plate in the center of the table held only a few crumbs. Doris brought over a fresh pot of coffee and we all took our places while Doris poured.

"I'm here, everyone!" A breathless Clarice rushed into the room. "Did you start already?"

"No, we waited for you." Doris looked around the table. "What's going on in the theater? Let's begin with Enid."

Enid's round face showed her frustration. "I didn't see too much of rehearsal, but Barbara Armstrong had the nerve to come into the paint shop to check on my set. She actually said that—to check on my set. I asked her how much construction experience she had—turned out none. I told her she could come back with the other volunteers when we were ready to paint. She didn't seem too enthusiastic."

"Well, I saw a lot of rehearsal," Margaret chimed in. "She sat next to Sebastian and was whispering in his ear constantly. It was nauseating. She got him water and coffee, asked if he wanted a more comfortable chair or a cushion. She was acting like a cross between the assistant director and Sebastian's personal gofer. Finally, Sylvia lost her temper and walked out. I heard her tell Sebastian that when he decided who was directing the play to let her know. Stephen is saying that he might be too busy to do hair and makeup. It's a shame. He was really excited to be working on a costume drama and he's so good you know he'd be up for an Encore Award."

Encore Awards were awarded for Excellence in Community Theater—somewhat of an oxymoron—but the awards themselves were highly coveted and given out at a lavish annual black tie ceremony.

"Are you saying that so far she's upset the scenic designer, the hair and makeup artist, the wardrobe mistress and the leading lady but Sebastian sees nothing wrong?"

Rose almost snarled at me, "Not to leave out both a very talented actress, and a costumer who refused to work in the same company as that woman."

Doris and I smiled at each other.

Margaret shook her head in disgust. "I've known Sebastian for years. He's a good director but insecure. That woman is a master manipulator. She had the nerve to ask me if the costumes I was designing were historically accurate. I asked her if she had a degree in costume design. She said no, so I said—well I do— which shut her up."

Frank joined in the discussion, "I was test painting one of the flats for Enid and that woman tried to tell me I was doing it wrong. I told her I only answered to the scenic designer and for her to get out of the paint shop. She's a real nasty one."

That shocked me. Frank was always the perfect gentleman. He hated any type of conflict.

Clarice spoke up, "That's why I'm here. I'm going to volunteer at the theater and become Bitch Barbara's best friend. I'll find out what her endgame is and report back to you. Sebastian can be an idiot at times, but he doesn't deserve to have that woman ruin this for him."

"What can she want with a theater group?" I was a little baffled. "In all the years I've known her she's never once shown any interest in amateur theater. She likes to run things, sit on boards, be in charge and tell people what to do."

Doris sniffed. "Since her husband left her, so have most of her friends. Maybe she's trying to find a new group of people to boss around."

Clarice chimed in again, "There's more to it than that. You all said that when Sebastian isn't around she acts as if she's the director. Everyone is really upset but Sebastian is oblivious. She's up to something and I'm going to find out what it is. My biggest worry is that some of the cast will quit the play. He has a lot of pressure on him to succeed with this one."

She glanced at her watch, "Come on, Frank. We've only got ten minutes before we open."

They both left for the library.

Doris shook her head. "She's going to ruin the play for him and he's too blind to see it." She sighed. "Well, I can't worry about that now. I've got to go down to the Senior Center."

"About school, Doris, it's not a game."

She placed her wrinkled hand over mine. "I know that, Kate. I told you, I'm not getting involved. But the people who know about this—" She put up her hand to silence me, then went on, "they're not just old people who don't know nothin' about nothin.' The Oppenheims worked for the FBI or something like that.

I don't think they were agents or spies or anything—but I don't know, they won't tell anyone what they did. They do know about secrecy. The other one—he's new at the Center—his name is Henry—is retired military who worked in security. The Oppenheims' grandson is going to help if they need him. He'll fit in with the students. Don't worry, Kate; they know what to look for."

She wiped the cake crumbs from her lap and stood. "Vincent said he's going to cut my grass one final time, and rake the rest of the leaves. Then he'll be studying for his Monday final."

Vincent not only drove me to school but he also insisted on working on any jobs Doris could find for him. I picked up my biology notes and went back to my apartment. I started at the first page. Half an hour later, I was only on the second page. The doorbell had rung and I went to answer the intercom only to discover my son-in-law was outside wanting to be let in.

He stomped into my apartment. "Ellie's asked for a divorce and it's your fault."

"Good morning to you, Andrew."

"I'm serious. Ellie just told me she wants a divorce and this never would have happened if you hadn't encouraged her to go back to school. This college thing is ridiculous…"

"Andrew, I have a final in two days. I don't have time for this infantile blame game. Say what you have to say and leave."

I was angry and it showed. He stalked over to the door and left, slamming it harder than necessary.

I went back to my text book and, of course, the front door bell rang again.

"Mom, it's me. I have to talk to you."

It was Ellie and she was furious. "I just saw Andrew leaving. What did he want?"

"He said you asked for a divorce and it's my fault."

"Your fault? How about…"

She plopped herself down in the armchair opposite the couch. "Let me tell you what happened last weekend. It was supposed to be our weekend away to discuss things. That didn't happen because we left the twins with Andrew's mother, although I told him that would be a mistake. We didn't even get to where we were going before she called to say the boys were acting up and we had to come home immediately. By the time we got there, everything was fine and they were already asleep, but it hardly mattered because Andrew had neglected to tell me that we were staying at some friends' cabin and the friends were going to be there too. He had no intention of discussing anything."

She scowled at me. "I'm done with Andrew. How in hell does he think he has the right to dictate to me what I can or can't do?"

I waited for the next onslaught. Ellie rarely lost her temper but when she did—watch out. I doubt Andrew had ever seen her in full offensive mode.

She put her hand out. "Give me the phone number for your divorce lawyer. I'll be talking to her as soon as my finals are over."

I meekly handed over the requested number. Ellie had on her mule face that brooked no argument.

"Ellie, have you discussed this with your father?"

"No, I already know what his reaction is going to be."

"He could maybe help you with the legalities," I tentatively offered.

"Mom, I said no. I don't need his help or opinion. I can handle this myself."

I thought it would be wise to change the subject. "Are you ready for finals?"

"Almost, though Andrew's done just about everything he could to sabotage my study time." She gave an exasperated sigh. "Do you think Doris could do some extra baby-sitting for me—just until finals are over?"

"I'm sure she could. Ellie, about the divorce…"

She put up her hand to stop me. "Right now, I want to pass my finals. I'll think about the divorce once they're over."

Chapter 18

Doris had called a meeting of her special ops group, so I invited Vincent to study in my apartment. I gave him the den and took the couch in the living room. After a couple of hours, I wandered into the kitchen to find something to eat. Vincent must have heard me and he followed me in.

"I'm through with studying."

"Me too," I answered. I was. I could almost quote the whole text book verbatim. If I didn't know the material by now I never would.

"You have two finals tomorrow, Vincent?"

"Yes, two tomorrow, one on Tuesday and, of course, American History on Wednesday."

We looked at each other and laughed. He said, "Thank you for letting me study up here—it's hard to concentrate downstairs—everyone's talking at the same time, though Henry seems to be taking control."

I sat down at the table after heating up some leftover lasagna and handing him a plateful. "Vincent, I'm worried about Doris' group. It seems as if it's some sort of game with them."

"Don't worry, Kate. Doris has sworn them to secrecy and they all have some kind of investigative background."

"Then you think it will go as planned?"

"I do. Doris has told them that it's a confidential stalking situation and they seem to have accepted that. Henry has pretty much taken over the planning—he has some kind of military experience—he won't say exactly what—but he's stressing low key, low profile and keeping in contact through text messages—that's if anyone will be able to read Doris'."

"Doris isn't supposed to be going anywhere near school."

"As far as I know, she isn't. But you know Doris."

I did.

He sat down opposite me. "Kate, I know they're all enjoying this a little too much but apart from Doris and the Oppenheims' grandson Peter, they all had either stimulating or dangerous jobs. I think they're finding it exciting."

"I just want to finish the semester and leave the investigating to Sam and company."

"Well, let's start quizzing each other because I'd love to catch the end of the Colt's game."

And we settled down to work.

Chapter 19

Vincent drove me to school for my biology exam. We agreed to meet in the cafeteria when we were finished. I looked around for someone who seemed to be taking an interest in me, but didn't see anyone watching or acting suspiciously. As promised, I didn't see Doris anywhere and I went to class wondering if the whole thing had fallen through.

I finished early, handed in my test paper and blue book then made my way to the cafeteria to wait for Vincent. As I stood by the door, scanning the room, I saw Ellie sitting at a table with a group of young people. They were all talking and laughing. It was the most animated I had seen Ellie since she'd graduated from high school.

I felt a sudden pang. This is what Ellie had missed by marrying so young. This was one reason she was so dissatisfied with her marriage. For the first time, I acknowledged her divorcing Andrew as a reality. It was sad when I thought of my grandsons being split between two parents. I had no doubt that Andrew loved them and Ellie too, but why couldn't the idiot realize that by trying to control her, he was pushing her further away.

Had I contributed to the dissension in their marriage by going back to school? I gave myself a mental shake—no, that was Andrew trying to make their marital problems my fault instead of his. In reality, Ellie had married too young and was now discovering how much she had missed by opting not to go to college.

The cafeteria was full, but just when I thought I would have to sit in the hallway outside, two students got up from a table. I hurried towards it and was about to sit when I realized that one of the chairs was still occupied.

"Are you waiting for someone or is this chair free?"

The older, well-groomed man with the Van Dyke beard stood up and answered me, "Please, sit down. I'm just taking a break before I proctor the next exam."

He waited until I sat then took the chair opposite me. He held out his hand. "I'm Dr. Cutler. I teach history, mostly early English up to medieval. Are you a student here?"

I took his hand. "I am. Kate Conley."

He leaned forward to shake my hand and I got a faint hint of aftershave—something spicy, but subtle, not cloying. His handshake was firm and warm.

"Majoring in?"

"Probably history and anthropology; I'm only a freshman so I'm not totally decided yet."

"Then maybe I'll see you in one of my classes next semester."

"What will you be teaching?"

"The Black Death and how it changed the social structure of England and Guy Fawkes and the Gunpowder Plot."

Both classes sounded fascinating.

He looked up. "There's my *compadre*—must be time to go."

A tall man with a shaggy beard and sandals loomed over me and grinned. "If old Neville there is trying to recruit you for one of his classes, I teach history too—Ancient Greece."

Dr. Cutler looked irritated.

The man leaned over the table and stuck out his hand, "Arthur Fleming and I hope to see you in one of my classes."

I watched them leave together, the neat, diminutive Dr. Cutler and the tall shambling Dr. Fleming. I was intrigued: plagues and politics, or Greek city states? The last thing I wanted was another Ted Thompson as a teacher. This time around I would do my research before I signed up for either class.

Chapter 20

That evening both Doris and Vincent came up to eat dinner with me.

"Did you see us?" Doris asked

"No, I was wondering if you'd cancelled the whole thing."

Doris grinned triumphantly. "Oh, we was there."

"Doris…"

"I had to—we was short a person. Henry said that sometimes the end justifies the means—he's real smart. Charlie and Frannie Oppenheim were sitting at the next table to you in the cafeteria and you didn't even notice them."

I had seen an older couple but they were completely engrossed in their books. Occasionally, they would lean across the table and point something out to the other. I never once saw them glance my way.

"Did you see me? I was in disguise sitting at the table in the corner. My subject was Ellie. Peter Oppenheim had her before and after her final. I took over once she was in the cafeteria waiting for the next exam. Vincent saw her back to her classroom—they both had the same class—then Peter Oppenheim followed her out to the parking lot and made sure she got to her car safely. Henry said we all did a great job and we're meeting at my place for a debriefing and instructions for Day Two early tomorrow morning."

Vincent grinned at me. "You and Sam will get a full report once the op is over. It was a lot of fun—like being real undercover operatives."

"I have to say, I never noticed any of you."

Vincent laughed as he and Doris high-fived.

Tuesday was almost a re-run of the previous day except that Ellie caught up with me in the cafeteria. "Mom, don't look now but you see that guy sitting over against the wall? I said not to look," she hissed as I immediately turned around. "I think he's stalking me. He followed me out to the parking lot yesterday and he's been following me today."

I took a discreet glance at the young man sitting at a small table against the wall. He was totally engrossed in his laptop.

"Are you sure? He seems to be studying."

"Just watch, Mom, and see if he follows me. Better yet, you're done for the day—why don't you let me drive you home?"

That would cause Doris' operatives to have a complete meltdown.

I quickly said, "Can't Ellie. Vincent drove me to school this morning and his phone's turned off while he's in class so I wouldn't be able to let him know."

She frowned. "Well, watch that guy and see what he does."

Just then Ellie's supposed stalker closed up his laptop and hurried from the cafeteria. I shrugged my shoulders. "Looks as if he's lost interest."

As Ellie gathered up her books, I noticed the same elderly man and woman from yesterday walk slowly past our table, ambling along chatting to each other. With a quick, "See you at home, Mom," Ellie slid past them and out the door. I noticed their pace quicken as she moved out of sight.

Just then I saw Vincent standing in the doorway. He waved to me and another day was over for the security detail.

Chapter 21

D-Day dawned. Doris and her operatives had an early meeting in her apartment. I wasn't invited.

"It's best you not be able to recognize anyone. Henry wants us to be totally *incognito*. That means anonymous," she declared triumphantly. "I'm beginning to think Henry was a spy. He sure seems to know a lot about undercover work. It's a lot of fun."

"Will you be at school this evening?"

Doris dropped her eyes. "I'm not allowed to say, Kate. If you do see me and I'm not saying you will, pretend not to notice me." She looked at her watch, "I've got to go. I invited our team back here after our op is over and I have food to fix. See you at school." She giggled, "Or maybe not."

My intercom buzzed. It was Sam. I knew as soon as he came in the door that he was stressed. "Kate, please be careful this evening. Kreutz and Hanley will be close by and I'll come straight to the school as soon as I can."

He started to say something else but instead gave me a fierce hug and immediately left. I pulled out the text book that I knew by heart and began reading again.

Vincent and I rode to school in silence. Since it was evening, the parking lot was only half full and we were able to park near Cavanaugh Hall. There were a few people milling around inside, but nobody except the other students in my class were familiar.

My creepy teacher handed out the test papers. It was a multiple choice exam and as I scanned it, I realized that I had over-prepared. Dr. Ted wasn't going to spend time reading essays, multiple choice was so much easier to grade. We were all cautioned to turn off our cell phones and within forty-five minutes, I was finished.

I placed my paper on the pile on his desk and without even a glance at him left the room and made my way to the cafeteria to wait for Vincent.

The room was empty. I'd ridden down in an empty elevator and now the cafeteria was empty, too. I sat at a table near the wall and took out my text book. I was pretty sure my test answers were correct but decided to check anyway.

There was a faint hint of spice with undertones of sandalwood, and a cultured voice said, "Hello there, Mrs. Conley. Are you finished with your final?"

I looked up to see Dr. Cutler, the English history professor standing next to my table.

"I'm waiting for my ride," I explained.

"Do you mind if I join you?"

I closed my book. "Please do."

He sat and we spent the next few minutes making small talk until he said something that made me sit up and take notice.

"How about a cup of coffee, or hot chocolate? Which will it be?"

I hesitated then answered, "Hot chocolate, please."

He chuckled. "Wise choice, the coffee is undrinkable." He walked over to the machine and stood there with his back towards me. In a couple of minutes, he returned and placed a cup in front of me.

This was what you might call a quandary. I hadn't seen any of Doris' 'operatives' but I could hardly refuse to drink from the cup he had put on the table. He held his cup up in a toast. "Here's to good grades on all your finals."

Before I had a chance to take a sip from mine, an old lady came wandering into the cafeteria. She was carrying a pile of books. As she passed the table, they slid from her arms and ended up on the floor right next to Dr. Cutler.

"Oh my," she twittered, "I'm ever so sorry. Did they fall on your foot?"

It was Doris but I almost didn't recognize her. She was dressed in a shapeless, baggy skirt that hung to her ankles topped with a strange psychedelic tee-shirt that I had never seen before. Her hair was long, straight and multi-colored, topped with a colorful scarf tied in a bow with the ends trailing down. There was a large fake flower stuck over one ear. If she was trying to look inconspicuous it wasn't working. She looked like a very elderly version of a Woodstock flower child.

Dr. Cutler helped her pick up her books and while his back was turned to me, I quickly switched our cups of hot chocolate. Doris left, still thanking and apologizing to him in her new hippie persona, "Thanks ever so much. I hope I didn't hurt your foot." She even raised her fingers as she exited the room, "Peace, brother."

I kept my composure and lifted my cup, "To perfect grades." We both slugged down our drinks and I waited for his reaction.

There wasn't one. He kept droning on about the Black Death. It was certainly his passion. We got past how the plague arrived in Europe, which must have taken at least thirty minutes—the description not the length of the journey—then I had to listen to his account of the various types of plague with the symptoms described in excruciating detail.

"There were three kinds of plague: bubonic, pneumonic and septicaemic."

And, of course, they all had different symptoms and causes. I glanced discreetly at my watch. Where was Vincent?

His depiction of the stinking, black buboes that covered the victims' bodies almost sent me over the edge, but I was saved by a stocky, gray-haired woman who came hurrying into the room.

"Neville, sorry I'm late. Traffic was terrible and it took longer than expected."

She hurried over to the table and started rearranging his pile of papers.

Dr. Cutler turned to me. "This is Stephanie. She works for me in the history department and she's my ride for today."

I must have looked surprised because he went on to explain, "I don't drive. I make do with public transportation. It's only a problem with evening events and then I either Uber or rely on the kindness of friends."

With barely a glance at me, Stephanie quickly grasped my hand and with a muttered, "Nice to meet you," she picked up his papers and led the way to the door.

He followed her, walking a perfectly straight line.

Chapter 22

"So Cutler isn't the accomplice?" Sam was saying.

"I guess not. He told me he doesn't drive, which must mean he doesn't own a car. He said he uses public transportation in the day and relies on cabs or ride-sharing for evening events."

"Who was the woman?"

"Stephanie. I didn't get the last name but she works in the history department."

Sam sighed. "It's so damned frustrating. We don't seem to be any closer to solving this case."

He had turned up on my doorstep last night, later than expected, and we were sitting at the kitchen table finishing up breakfast.

I heard the ping of his phone. He glanced down at it. "Gotta go, Kate."

He took a last swig of coffee and crammed the remains of a toasted bagel into his mouth.

As he shrugged into his jacket, I asked, "What about the latest missing girl? Do you have any leads?"

"No, but Claire Richardson, the one who was in ICU, called me while I was on the road yesterday and wants to come in and talk with me. She's remembered something more. That was her, texting. She's waiting at the station for me."

The minute he went clattering down the stairs, Doris was at my front door.

"Kate, what did you think of my disguise yesterday?"

"I didn't recognize you at first. You made a great hippie."

She laughed. "It was exciting. I loved doing it. I think I would have made a good spy."

"Ellie noticed the Oppenheim's grandson following her. He was in the cafeteria, but left before she did. I saw the Oppenheims walking behind her as she went to the parking lot. She didn't even see them."

Doris poured herself a cup of coffee. "I don't think Henry is done with the case. He wants to know a lot more about it. He keeps asking me about the stalker."

"There isn't a stalker."

"I know, but I had to have some explanation for our op. Trouble is he wants to find him and there's nothing to find."

"Sam's still working on the kidnapped girls. He said…" I stopped. I was so used to confiding in Doris that it was hard to remember to keep things from her.

She leaned over and patted my hand. "It's all right, honey. I know there's things you can't tell me."

"I wish you wouldn't tell me what you're doing either, unless I can tell Sam. By keeping things from him, I feel as if as if I'm lying to him."

"Hmm, then I won't tell you anything so there'll be nothin' to keep from Sam. And I don't want to know anything confidential because then I'll have to keep it from the troops." She shrugged her shoulders at my inquiring look. "That's what we call each other. I will tell you one more thing then we're not going to mention it again. Henry still wants to meet as a group."

"But school's out until the end of January. What will you investigate?"

She shook her head. "I should never have lied about the stalker. He's determined to find him and he's not a man who gives up easily."

"So what are you going to do?"

"I've got an idea."

"Which is?"

Doris refused to answer me.

By which I deduced it was something I couldn't tell Sam, which meant it was something I should worry about.

Chapter 23

Kate, can you meet me for lunch?

It was a text from Sam. I hadn't seen or heard from him since yesterday morning when he'd told me that the kidnapped girl who'd escaped had remembered something more about her time in captivity. I texted back a *yes*.

We met at the new restaurant near the hospital. Sam was already sitting at a table. He rose to greet me. As we sat down, I noticed an elderly man shuffle over and sit behind us, even though the dining room was almost empty and he had his choice of tables.

"You know I never told you what Claire said."

It took a moment for me to recollect that Claire was the kidnapped girl who had spent weeks in ICU after being found in a ditch out in the wilds of Shelby County.

"How is she? Did she remember anything else?"

"She's recovered well. She's a very smart girl. Not only did she not eat or drink anything after the first day because she realized the food and water was drugged, but she pretended to be ill. The kidnapper dragged her outside and put her in the trunk of his car before driving to a cornfield to dump her. She counted time elapsed, every turn on the road and as far as she could tell, the type of road surface, so now we're backtracking from where she was found and hopefully, we'll find the Quonset hut."

"Quonset hut?"

"That's where she said she was held, in an old Quonset hut. It was in some woods and she saw no other buildings nearby."

Sam took a large bite of his sandwich and washed it down with half a cup of coffee. "She told me she heard no traffic or other sounds when she was in the car trunk so it must have been in a secluded part of the county. That's what we're doing now, reversing her directions and checking every dirt road or track we come across to get back to the place she was held." He sighed, "We have to find the latest kidnapped girl as soon as possible. Her mother tells us she has asthma and since her inhaler was found in her backpack at school it could be a dangerous situation for her."

"Do you know when she was taken?"

"As far as we can determine, the same day as your attempted kidnapping."

"Sam, do you think she was the girl in the janitor's closet?"

"More than likely. Anyway, I didn't want to talk to you about that. I missed you at school and wanted to talk about how the evening of your final went. We didn't have much time yesterday morning."

"My final was very short and easy. When I went to the cafeteria to wait for Vincent, it was empty until Dr. Cutler turned up. I didn't see any of Doris' special ops people so when he offered to get me a cup of hot chocolate from the machine I was a little perturbed but luckily Doris turned up..."

Sam almost exploded. "What the hell was Doris doing there? You told me she was staying away from school."

"That's what she said and I believed her."

He calmed down a little. "So, what happened?"

"She told me they were short a person so she had to fill in."

'I mean with the hot chocolate?"

"When Dr. Cutler set the cup in front of me and proposed a toast to good grades, I didn't know how to get out of drinking it, but then Doris came in. She was in disguise." I was going to describe Doris' hilarious, hippie outfit but Sam didn't seem in the mood to appreciate the humor, so I hurriedly went on, "She had an armful of books that she dropped at his feet and in the confusion, I switched cups."

"And he drank it?"

"We both did."

"But it wasn't drugged?"

"Couldn't have been. We went on talking and he left under his own steam."

Sam was lost in thought for a moment. He checked his watch. "I gotta go.' He rose from the table then turned back to me. "One more thing. You said Cutler didn't drive."

"That's what he said. Some woman turned up all apologetic because she was late. He introduced her as Stephanie from the history department and said she was his ride."

"And that's when he told you he didn't drive, right?"

"Right, mostly he rides the bus and when he has evening events, he relies on friends for transportation."

"Okay. I'll try to text when I can, but we'll be driving all over the county again trying to find the Quonset hut."

He dropped a brief kiss on my cheek and hurried out.

I took a deep breath. I felt as if I'd avoided a catastrophe. Sam was adamant that neither Doris nor I should get involved in his case.

"Excuse me."

The old man at the next table was standing at my side. In a meek, quavering voice he said, "I'm ever so sorry. I hope you don't think me rude but I couldn't help overhearing your conversation."

I was going to retort something along the lines of 'especially since you chose to sit at the table right next to us' but he looked like such a frail, timid creature that I didn't want to hurt his feelings.

He went on, "Do you mind if I join you for a moment. I'm Henry, a friend of Doris'."

"Oh please, sit."

He winced slightly as he carefully eased into the chair opposite me.

I waved the server over. "I'm going to have another cup of coffee. Would you like to join me?"

"Yes but decaf for me, please. Heart you know— have to be careful."

So this fragile man was the famous Henry—the ex-spy?

He coughed slightly. "I just wanted to know if everything is resolved with the stalker case. Do you need any more help from us?"

He looked as if I could push him over with one finger, but I refrained from laughing and said, "No, I'm pretty certain that's the last we've heard of the stalker."

He looked relieved. "Oh good, because Doris has another case for us."

"She does?"

"It's something to do with the theater. Doris calls it the Bitch Barbara dilemma." He dropped his eyes with embarrassment. "Sorry, I shouldn't have called her that."

"That's alright, Mr..?"

"Oh, please, just call me Henry." He cleared his throat, "Do you mind a few questions, Mrs. Conley?"

Two cups of coffee later, after he had asked me how I knew Barbara Armstrong, I found I had shared with him my marriage and contentious divorce, my relationship with Sam, my broken leg, my sleazy little history teacher and everything I knew about our local community theater and Bitch Barbara.

I felt guilty for monopolizing the conversation but Henry sat there quietly, asked the occasional question and listened patiently to my answers. I decided he was a sad old man who was lonely and willing to listen to anyone. Later, I changed my mind. Henry had hidden depths. I had shared my life history with him but hadn't even learned his last name.

Chapter 24

After I got back from lunch with Sam, I found Ellie waiting for me. As soon as I walked through the door, she started sobbing. Ellie never cried and it was some time before I could get a coherent word out of her. Finally, she calmed down enough to be able to answer the questions I threw at her.

"It's Andrew. He's fighting the divorce. He said if I go ahead with it he's going to ask for sole custody of the boys and he's refusing to pay any kind of support. Can he do that? He's closed our joint checking account. I have no money at all."

I felt my blood pressure rising. "No, he can't do that, Ellie."

"But he's already done it." Ellie almost wailed. "The credit cards are cancelled and all our bank accounts. He told me if I want to get a divorce, I'll have to pay for it myself."

"You need to talk to your father."

She looked at me with tear-swollen eyes. "I already have. He agrees with Andrew. He said he was far too lenient with you when you divorced."

Sure Jack was lenient—he had little choice. I had walked in and caught him on top of his desk in the law office. His young, blond personal assistant was also on the desk—underneath Jack. I'd attacked him with one of his own golf clubs which he had conveniently left by the office door. My arrest for assault made the front page of the *Shelbyville News*. Jack had been hoping for a quiet, discreet divorce, but the ensuing publicity put paid to that and to his hopes of being elected to the school board, another of his ambitions.

My lawyer pointed out that I had quit college and worked two jobs to put Jack through law school. I'd also worked in the office full-time plus had another part-time job for the first few years. I was awarded a very generous settlement plus half the profits from the business of which I was co-owner.

Ellie's eyes filled with tears again. "Andrew is forcing me to stay in the marriage by withholding all support and threatening me with the loss of my children. I thought Dad would understand my point of view and help me, but instead of calling Andrew out for the bully he is, he's supporting him."

I tried to stay calm. "What does *your* lawyer say?"

"I haven't spoken to her yet. Andrew said we could settle it by ourselves."

I picked up the phone and immediately made an appointment for Ellie the next day.

"Do you want me to go with you tomorrow?"

She nodded yes.

"Make a list of all the assets you remember, get documentation if you can and also the exact date when Andrew decided to withhold support. We're not letting him get away with this. I'll go talk to your father right away." I comforted her as best I could and she left in a calmer frame of mind.

When I got to the office, I found Jack in conference with a client so spent the waiting time talking with his secretary, Sarah something. I'd only met her once before and that was after Jack had divorced the bimbo and hired her as his new assistant. That day he had asked to meet with me at the office where he had the effrontery to ask if we could remarry.

The answer was a decided *hell no.* The discussion escalated when I elaborated on my answer and a blindly furious Jack, in his haste to get rid of me, walked into his door. He blamed me for the resulting broken nose.

I had found his new employee smothering her laughter in the outer office. By the way she high-fived me as I was leaving, I gathered she was not a fan of her new boss.

Now she was decidedly friendly. "Mrs. Conley, I wonder if I could talk to you, privately..." She broke off as Jack's door opened and he followed his client out.

A look of fear shot across his face—hardly surprising given our volatile history.

He cleared his throat nervously, "Do you have an appointment?"

"Of course I don't," I snapped back. "I have something to discuss with you."

He looked guilty. "I'm sorry. I have another client."

His secretary interjected, "He just called, sir. He's going to be a few minutes late."

Jack glared at her. I didn't wait for more excuses. I stalked ahead of him and seated myself opposite his desk.

He followed me in. "What is it?"

"It's Ellie. You probably know her marriage is on the rocks and she and Andrew are getting a divorce."

"It's absolutely ridiculous. Why would she even think of divorce?"

"Maybe because Andrew is forbidding her to go to school." I emphasized *forbidding*. "Now he says he won't pay her fees and wants full custody of the boys."

Jack cleared his throat nervously. "Why does she need a college education?"

"Because, if her husband decides to cheat on her she'll have to have a career to support herself."

"Andrew isn't going to cheat on her."

"Really? Isn't that exactly what you did when I gave up my college education to marry you and put you through law school? Ellie's being a little more proactive than I was."

Jack wouldn't look at me. He started re-arranging papers on his desk. Getting no answer, I went on, "Anyway, since we didn't pay for Ellie's college after she graduated from high school, I thought we could share the cost now."

Jack got up from his chair and paced the room. "No, I can't do that. Business is down. I can't afford it."

"Even if things are slow right now it still shouldn't be a problem for either of us. IUPUI is hardly an expensive school."

"No, I won't do it." He stood. "I have someone waiting and I don't want to hear any more on the subject."

He picked up the phone. "Is my next client here?" Turning to me, he said, "I'm sorry but you'll have to leave."

I was stunned. Jack wouldn't even discuss this? "You do know that Ellie won't forgive you for this. She will never forget that you supported Andrew over her, your own daughter."

A look of sadness crossed his face— Ellie and Jack had always been close. His eyes filled with tears. He blinked them away and gruffly reiterated, "You have to go."

I didn't move. He wasn't going to get rid of me that easily. "Since I'm here, let's discuss why revenues are down."

He froze. "That's none of your business."

"Since I own half of this, it is my business."

The phone interrupted what was starting to be a very contentious discussion. He picked it up with a look of relief on his face. "My next client is here."

I turned on my heels and walked out, almost running down the anxious looking, middle-aged man being ushered into the office. As I opened the outer door to leave, Sarah stopped me. "Mrs. Conley?"

I paused in my angry dash out the door. I must have looked surprised because she cleared her throat. "There's something I'd like to discuss with you…"

Jack's door opened and he barked out, "I need the Simpson file."

She hurriedly broke off. "Goodbye, Mrs. Conley." She turned towards the filing cabinet. As she moved past me, she quietly muttered, "I'll call you later."

Chapter 25

I was too furious to go home What I really needed was to run around the high school track a few times until the blazing anger inside me subsided into a flickering flame. Unfortunately the boot on my broken ankle prohibited that. So I did the next best thing and headed for the library to spend two or three hours mindlessly shelving books.

As I walked through the beautifully carved doors, the hushed library enfolded me in its soothing peace. I could feel my breathing slow as I signed in, wheeled my cart of books into the stacks, and emptied my mind of everything but the job at hand. The serenity of the old building flowed around me and I felt my body relax into an almost meditative state.

My calm was shattered by a high pitched, little voice calling my name, "Mrs. Conley, Mrs. Conley."

I hauled myself to my feet and looked for the source of the interruption. At first I didn't recognize her. It had been almost a year since I'd set foot in our local theater. Her hair was styled differently and she seemed taller than I remembered, but I finally dredged up her name from the recesses of my mind. "Cindy, how nice to see you again."

It was the young assistant stage manager who had worked on the first and only production in which I'd appeared at our community theater.

"Could I talk to you?"

"Of course."

I led her over to a deserted corner where we could have some privacy. "What is it?"

She stood quietly twisting her hands together, then took a big gulp and let everything flow out. "Sebastian's angry with me because he thinks I messed up the props. Two of them were missing, the tray and sherry glasses for the second scene and the writing case and pen. I told him I'd set them. And I did—I really did—I always set the table and then double check with the props list."

I thought back to the one play I'd appeared in. Cindy had seemed to be everywhere backstage, setting the various items the actors needed on the prop table in the wings. Since the actors were also served a part of a formal dinner as part of the stage business, it was an extremely labor intensive play for all involved. Despite the complexity of the job, during the whole run of the show she had never once made a mistake. In fact, Sebastian had bragged to me how lucky he had been to acquire such a gem.

Now her face reflected the anger she felt. "I never make a mistake. Doris tried to cover for me, and Tim, who's playing *Dr. Sloper,* said it didn't matter. But I knew I'd set both of them. Somebody must have moved them. Sebastian sent his new assistant or whatever she's supposed to be, to check, and she said they were still in the prop room on the shelf. Mrs. Conley, I know they were on the table but he wouldn't believe me." Her eyes filled with tears. "He yelled at me. I love working at the theater but it's no fun anymore. Today I'm going to tell him I quit."

Sebastian crossed the end of the stacks. He stopped when he saw us. Cindy straightened up. "Might as well get it over with."

Sebastian started to move away but she stopped him. They had a brief conversation. I saw Sebastian try to interrupt, but Cindy waved her finger in his face as she threw one more remark at him. She turned away and walked out of the library, every inch of her body reflecting the anger she felt. Sebastian watched her leave. His shoulders slumped and he moved slowly out of sight.

I went back to my cart and quietly worked until it was time to leave.

On my way out, I passed the librarian's desk. Sylvia was sitting there lost in thought. She looked up as I went by, "Hi, Kate. Did you hear? Cindy just quit. Now we have to find a new assistant stage manager on top of everything else."

"Things are not going well?"

"Ever since he let that woman into the company people have been leaving the show. I'm thinking of it myself. Stephen is no longer doing hair and makeup. Margaret is arguing with Sebastian over the costumes. If she quits, Frank will quit. It's almost as if Barbara Armstrong is trying to sabotage the show, but Sebastian refuses to admit he's wrong about her."

Doris was waiting for me as I started up the back stairs. "Did you hear what's happening at the theater?" She pulled me into her kitchen. "Do you think they'll be able to replace everyone who's leaving?"

"I'm beginning to feel sorry for Sebastian."

Doris set her mouth. "It's his own fault, Kate."

"I know, but he's such a good kind person he doesn't understand someone as nasty and manipulative as Bitch Barbara. It's sad; he was so excited at finally getting his choice of play to direct and I'm afraid it's going to be a complete flop."

I turned down Doris' invitation to dinner, pleading a headache and wearily dragged myself up the stairs to my own apartment. The day had been an utter disaster. I collapsed onto the couch. Digger walked over to me and rested his head on my knee. I rubbed his droopy ears and he licked my hand. I kissed the top of his head and relaxed. What would I do without Digger?

Chapter 26

My day started with a call from Ellie. "Mom, I've cancelled my lawyer's appointment."

"Why?"

I was almost ready to leave to pick her up and was spending the last few minutes looking through my own divorce papers.

I could tell by the tremor in her voice she was stressed. "She wants me to bring all the financial information, bank account numbers—things like that—but I can't find one single piece of paper relating to our finances. Everything is gone including our taxes for the past five years. Andrew kept everything in his desk but it's empty." Her voice cracked and I knew she was close to tears. "The lawyer asked if we had a safety deposit box, but I couldn't answer her. I left all that to Andrew. I feel so stupid."

"Don't worry about it, Ellie. You can get copies. Andrew's trying to make things more difficult for you. Your lawyer will know all the steps to take."

After she hung up, I went downstairs to talk to Doris but she was in a hurry to get rid of me. "The troops are coming over to talk about you-know-who and I have to fix some biscuits and gravy. I know you don't want to sit in with the group because there may be something that Sam shouldn't know about."

More likely it was something he should.

My phone rang again and I picked it up without checking caller ID.

"It's me, Sarah," a voice whispered. "I'm in the office so I might have to hang up. Can we meet tonight at 6.30?"

"Sure." I replied.

"Let's go to the Bluebird Restaurant on Main Street in Morristown. It's not that far and their fried chicken and strawberry-rhubarb pie is the best in town." I was going to ask for directions but there was a sharp intake of breath, a quick, *gotta go,* and she hung up in my ear. Morristown was a twenty minute drive and there were plenty of out of the way places to eat in Shelbyville. Sarah definitely did not want to be seen with me.

When I arrived at the restaurant, she was waiting at a table in the back of the room. We ordered and I let her finish her dinner before asking any questions. We had eaten in almost complete silence until Sarah wiped her fingers and pushed her empty plate to one side. She was right about the fried chicken. It was the best I'd tasted outside Doris' kitchen.

"I couldn't help but hear Mr. Conley tell you that business is down this year." She waited for my reply.

"I was surprised to hear that."

Sarah exhaled sharply. "The books used to be kept in the filing cabinets up front behind my desk, but they disappeared from there. Now they're in Mr. Conley's safe in his office. I don't have the combination for that."

"But I do," I answered.

She looked down before saying, "I just wanted you to know. I know the new accountant is your son-in-law but..."

"What!" I grabbed her arm. "Say that again!"

"About your son-in-law? You didn't know?"

"I knew Robert Armstrong had been replaced. I had no idea that it was by my daughter's husband."

Robert was Bitch Barbara's ex-husband. Well, more or less—the divorce would be final any day. He had been our accountant almost since the office opened. In fact, he was still my personal accountant. When I received my last quarterly income check from the business, I had deposited it in my bank account and sent the paperwork to Robert. It was only recently that I realized it was for a considerably smaller amount than usual.

Sarah took a deep breath. "Something's not right with the books. Mr. Conley left the safe unlocked a couple of weeks ago when he was at one of his meetings. So I looked at them." She shrugged her shoulders. "I wanted to know why he locked them up. We had a couple of big clients recently and I know their bills have been paid because I handle the mail and make the bank deposits. There was no sign of the payment in the books I looked at. I went back a few months and it was the same thing, bills that I know had been paid were not listed. It looks as if revenues have been under reported since the beginning of the year."

I sat back in my chair. "And all this started after Robert Armstrong quit and Andrew Fisher took over?"

"Exactly, but there's more. There's another set of books in the bottom of the safe."

"Are they the same as the first?"

"I don't know. I didn't have time to look. I heard Mr. Conley's car outside so I put everything back and left the safe open as I found it."

"So you think they're keeping a double set of books?"

"I'm saying it's a possibility and that maybe you should check."

I smiled. "You keep my ex-husband's calendar, don't you?"

"I do."

"So you know when he'll be in the office and more importantly, when he won't be."

Sarah nodded.

"And, unless he's changed the combination, I can open his safe."

"I'll help. You'll need to make copies of everything."

My mouth dropped open. I wasn't expecting Sarah to be any further involved.

"Mrs. Conley, it'll be faster with both of us there. Besides I don't like the new accountant. He's a real jerk and I'd love for him to get his come-uppance."

"Sorry," she said belatedly, evidently remembering he was my son-in-law. She leaned across the table, "Let's do it as soon as possible. We can sneak in one night after hours."

"And he'll never know we've been there."

We grinned at each other. Instead of the strawberry-rhubarb pie, we ordered two large glasses of wine, raised them in a toast then started making our plans.

Chapter 27

The more I thought about Andrew and Jack conspiring to cheat me out of my share of revenue from the business, the angrier I became. When I added in Andrew's treatment of Ellie and the fact that my sleazy ex-husband was helping him, that put paid to any sleep for me that night. By morning, I was ready to take revenge.

Sam stopped by to share a cup of coffee with me before another long day of driving around Shelby County. I debated telling him about Jack and Andrew, but decided against it. He was already stressed about the kidnapped girl's health since she suffered from asthma.

"Her parents are beside themselves, not only because of not knowing where she is, but because Claire told them she smelled mold in the Quonset hut and that could definitely trigger an attack."

As I refilled his coffee cup, Sam gently laid his hand over mine, "What's wrong, Kate? You seemed distracted this morning."

I leaned against him. Sam always felt warm and comforting—a human version of Digger. "It's Ellie. She and Andrew are having problems. I'll fill you in on everything later." I didn't want to share my plans for breaking into Jack's safe to copy his books. I also didn't want Sam to know that I was involving the office secretary in my faintly illicit scheme. *Not illicit, not even faintly*, I told myself. *I was part owner of the business. I had a perfect right to examine the books whenever I wanted.* Even if that meant I had to sneak around at night to do it.

"What are your plans for today?"

"Claire has suggested that she ride with us. She thinks if she sits in the back of the car with her eyes closed, she might be able to remember how fast the car was going and count off the seconds driven before each turn. It's worth a shot. Right now, it feels as if we're driving aimlessly around country roads and getting nowhere."

He checked his watch. "Time to go. Kate, if it's not too late, can I come over tonight? We haven't seen much of each other lately." He added gruffly, "I miss you," and pulled me close.

"I miss you too, but I might have plans for tonight."

"Oh?"

He waited, but I didn't add anything.

I kissed him. "Stay safe, Sam."

He gave me another hug and left down the back stairs.

He's got a meeting at his church tonight. Let's park at the deli and walk to the office.

So it was on. My stomach did a little flip. I texted back *ok* and spent the rest of the afternoon in an absolute funk. We were going into my ex-husband's office to open his safe and copy any confidential documents we could find.

What if he had changed the combination? He had always used the date that we met at college, all those years ago. Surely he'd changed it after the divorce? But maybe not, Jack had a hard time remembering numbers. He liked to stick with something familiar. I took a deep breath. I would soon find out.

What do you wear for an illicit operation? Black, for sure! I stood in front of my open closet and checked my wardrobe. Black pants, a black sweater, gloves—black of course—and what could I use to cover my face and hair?

The doorbell rang. I almost jumped out of my skin. It was Doris.

"Did I interrupt something?"

My heart was racing. "No, I wasn't expecting anyone."

She looked at me intently. "What's wrong, Kate?"

"I—I…"

There was no way I could lie to Doris. She walked into the kitchen, put the kettle on for tea and sat down at the table.

"Tell me what's going on."

And so I did. I started with Ellie's divorce, her missing documents, the altered books, and by the time I got to my planned break-in of Jack's office, Doris had slid a steaming cup of tea in front of me along with a plate of chocolate chip cookies she had brought up the day before.

"You know what you need," she said firmly, "a lookout."

I was horrified. "No, no—absolutely not. You can't get involved."

It was bad enough that Sarah was coming with me. There was no way Doris was going to come too.

She patted my hand. "I have the perfect disguise. Drink your tea and I'll be up a little later."

"Doris, no."

She waved my concerns away. "Don't worry. This isn't the first undercover op I've been on." And she disappeared down the back stairs.

I was ready and dressed in all black—except for my hair and face—when the front door opened and an old, bag lady wandered in. She was wearing down-at-heel boots with shapeless, baggy socks spilling over the tops and a shabby black skirt that I remembered from her hippy persona at school. An old darned, woolen sweater was covered by a man's flannel shirt missing half its buttons, with a shapeless cardigan, dotted with moth holes, and, ironically, smelling of particularly pungent moth balls, enveloping the entire outfit. Her hair was a long tangled mess that stuck out from under a scruffy, woolen cap. She was carrying a plastic garbage bag filled with heaven knows what. Doris grinned at me, exposing a mouthful of rotten teeth. Her wizened hands with their filthy, cracked nails were covered with dirt.

"This is my favorite disguise. Pretty good, huh, Kate?"

She handed me a black, woolen hat. "It's a balaclava."

"A what?"

"Just pull it over your head and all that shows is your eyes."

I put it on as instructed and discovered it was nothing more than a ski mask. "Doris, what do you plan on doing?"

"There's always some homeless hanging around the Square. I'm going to mingle with them. If I see anyone going towards the office door, I'll text you so you can get out fast."

I shook my head in exasperation. Doris had made up her mind she was coming and there was no way I could stop her. For better or for worse, Doris was now part of our burglary op.

It was almost time to go.

Chapter 28

Mr. Conley's meeting starts at 7. I'll meet you then. Don't take main roads, there could be cameras.

I texted back and went downstairs to pick up my bag lady accomplice. Doris grinned at me, a grotesque sight with her blacked-out teeth. "Don't forget to take the back streets—we don't want any of them police cameras checking your license plate. Although," she continued, "we could cover it up with mud."

I tried not to roll my eyes. Was I the only one who wasn't an expert on how to avoid detection? I needed to watch more television crime shows.

We parked on a side street next to the Square. "Not there," Doris cautioned. "Too close to that street light. I'll go on ahead. We shouldn't be seen together."

As I moved the car, she wandered towards a small knot of people sitting in the alley around the side of the deli. I had a moment of panic. There were some pretty shady-looking characters in the group. I quickly parked and hurried over to tell Doris she would have to wait in the car, when a heavy-set, older man with a ruddy complexion, took her arm. "Hello, Myrtle. I ain't seen you for a while. Come say 'hi' to the gang."

I was about to take her other arm and indulge in a game of tug o' war when I recognized some of the gang members. Prominent among them were the Oppenheims sitting on an old piece of cardboard with their backs against the brick wall of the building.

I gave up. Jack's office was on the next street and his back door on the 'alley of the homeless' as I dubbed it. I pulled my balaclava over my face, checked for street cameras and, keeping to the shadows, hurried towards Jack's office door.

I huddled under the porch looking around for Sarah.

"I'm over here," someone hissed.

She was crouched down under an old lilac bush. I unlocked the office door and she hurriedly crossed in front of me and entered the building. I had forgotten to ask if the office now included any kind of security system, but since no blaring alarm was triggered, I guessed not. Of course, if Jack ever learned about this little caper, it would be installed first thing.

We stood in the middle of the outer office and reconnoitered. Light spilled in through the windows from the street. It was enough that we wouldn't be tripping over anything in the dark. I heard footsteps outside and momentarily panicked but they passed on by and I released the breath I had been holding.

Sarah gave me a shaky smile. "Let's try the safe."

We tiptoed into Jack's office and looked around. The safe was in the same place it had originally occupied thirty years ago. I crouched in front of it, had a moment of panic when my mind went blank and I couldn't remember the combination, took a deep breath and spun the dial. I seized the handle, pulled it down and tugged. The heavy door swung open.

Sarah, high-fived me and turned on the copier while I examined the contents of the safe. I handed the first stack of account books I found to her, and heard the chug of the copier as it started to spit out its sheets of paper.

There were three large manila envelopes on the bottom shelf of the safe. I set them to one side to get at the other account books hidden underneath. They looked identical to the books Sarah was now busily copying. The noise of the copier was loud in the hushed, empty office and my heart thudded in my chest every time we heard a footstep outside. Finally she was done. She refilled the paper tray, handed me some envelopes and I gave her the second set of books.

I put the stapled sheets in one of the envelopes and waited for the next set. The first stack of books, I started to place on top of the three large manila envelopes ready to put them back in the safe in the exact order we had taken them out. I looked at them more closely. Surely, that was Andrew's hand-writing? It was. And inside each envelope was part of the missing banking information, with taxes and receipts stapled together and sorted by month. Andrew was making this easy for me.

The second batch of books was soon finished and Sarah had her hand out for the manila envelopes.

I cautioned her, "This is my son-in-law and daughter's financial information. I can't ask you to copy it, but since I will have my daughter's permission, I think it's legal for me to do it."

Actually, I wasn't sure if that was correct, but this was Ellie's information as well as Andrew's, so I threw any scruples to the winds.

Sarah handed me the copies of the second set of books and took the rest of the information from my hands. "Let me do it."

We were working like a well-oiled machine. While she took care of the copying, I put the stapled sheets into the appropriate envelopes. We were getting a large stack of information.

Finally, she took a deep breath and said, "I hope Mr. Conley doesn't keep track of the number of copies. I've printed more tonight than in the last three months."

She speedily filled the paper tray and shut the copier down.

I picked up the stack of envelopes while she made sure everything was as Jack had left it. We hurried through to the front office. We were about to open the outer door when my phone pinged with an incoming text.

hes coMinNoow.

It was too late to get out of the door. We heard footsteps outside then the sound of a key in the lock. In total panic, we quickly looked around and dived under the desk just as the door started to open, squeezing in as far as possible.

It was Jack.

Chapter 29

Sarah's nails were digging painfully into my arm and there was nothing I could do about it. I was afraid to move a muscle.

Jack was in the middle of a phone call as he entered the office. He sounded irritated.

"Why the hell did you leave your financial information in my safe anyway?" He listened for a few more seconds. "All right, all right I'll bring them." Then, "I don't have time for this."

We breathed a sigh of relief. If Jack was in a hurry maybe he wouldn't go near the copier. He wasn't the most observant of men, but surely even he would notice the heat radiating from the over-worked copy machine. We heard him cross the floor and the light clicked on in his office. Sarah stifled a squeak of alarm as we heard the dial spin on Jack's safe. We must have done a good job replacing everything because the safe door slammed shut, the light was switched off and Jack crossed to the outer door, opened it and left.

My legs were cramping and I crawled out of our hiding place and shakily stood. Neither of us could utter a word. I turned too quickly towards the door and as I did, dropped the pile of envelopes I was carrying. I heard the key in the office door once again.

We were caught. There was no way I could pick up the envelopes before Jack came in. Sarah and I gazed at each other in horror.

"Get back under the desk," I whispered, "No sense in his catching both of us."

Then I heard a plaintive lament, "I only need ten dollars, mister."

Jack's irritated voice replied, "Go away, I'm in a hurry."

"Just ten dollars. That will get me a bed for the night."

I heard a hysterical, "What about me?"

"Myrtle needs a bed too. Can you make it a twenty?"

"Yeah mister." It was Doris, "My arthuritis is playing up real bad. You wouldn't let an old lady like me sleep on a park bench would you?"

We frantically scrambled around, picked up the dropped envelopes and dashed to the back door in Jack's office. Myrtle and her friend were still pestering Jack and he was starting to lose his temper.

"Get the hell away from me before I call the police."

Sarah tried the door. She was panic stricken. "It's locked. I don't have a key. Do you?"

"Not to this door," I whispered back.

The front door opened. Jack was still talking on the phone. "If you wanted me to bring the other set of books, you should have told me." He walked across the floor, getting closer by the second. "I don't give a damn about your safety deposit box. Why can't both sets of books stay in my safe?"

He paused to listen. The answer must have been convincing because he gave an exasperated, "I've got the envelopes. I'll bring the second set of books, too."

There was nowhere to go but, just as Jack's back was turned to us and his hand went up to the light switch, the door we were leaning against silently opened outward. We almost fell into the alley. A hand dragged us through and it closed immediately. The heavy set man with the red face pushed us out of sight into the next doorway. The back door opened again. A puzzled looking Jack poked his head out, checked up and down the alley then slammed it shut.

"Did you get what you needed?" the man whispered.

I could barely answer but managed to squeak out a strangled 'yes'. My legs felt like rubber. I stumbled around the corner to the car with Sarah hanging onto my arm. Doris, AKA Myrtle, hurried towards us and the crowd of homeless melted away into the darkness. The heavy set man had disappeared.

On the drive home, I could barely function. That was way too close a call. Still, I had the copies of the books I needed, plus Andrew's purloined financial information. The timing had been perfect. If we'd waited a few minutes longer, it all would have been gone.

The only other close call was when I parked the car in the garage and Doris and I were walking towards the house. Sam's SUV pulled up outside the gate.

"Kate!" he yelled. "We did it! We found her. Claire's directions led us straight to the Quonset hut. The girl's in the hospital now but she's going to be okay."

He hot-footed it towards us and abruptly stopped when he saw me in my burgling outfit, accompanied by a homeless bag-lady.

"What the hell! Kate, what is this?"

Doris was the first to recover. "Hi, Sam, we went to a fancy dress party. What do you think of our costumes?" She grabbed the pile of envelopes out of my hand, dropped them into her garbage bag and gave me a hug. "Thanks for carrying my stuff. See you in the morning."

And she trotted towards the back door. As a bemused Sam climbed the back stairs, I looked behind me to see a grinning Doris flash a thumbs-up as she disappeared inside her apartment.

Chapter 30

The next morning my phone rang. It was Doris, "Is he there?"

I started to say, "No, he's in the shower..." when Sam walked into the kitchen clad in only a towel.

"Call you later, Doris."

She hurriedly said, "Got it, but I've a lot to tell you about these books." She hung up.

Sam poured himself a cup of coffee and sat down at the table. He said casually, "You and Doris had really good costumes for your party last night. Where was it held?"

I slid a couple of bagels into the toaster before answering. He was smiling, but his piercing blue eyes were ice cold and boring into mine.

Honesty seemed to be the best policy. I couldn't tell Sam that I broke into my ex-husband's law office, but I couldn't lie to him either.

"Sam, we didn't go to a party last night, but I don't want to tell you what we did."

"Because...?"

'I don't think you would approve and I don't want us to get into a big fight."

A pulse in his jaw started to throb, "Was it something illegal?"

"No, at least I don't think so. Please don't ask me about it."

"Did it involve just you and Doris?"

"I can't answer that, Sam. You'll have to trust me. I'll tell you when I can."

Luckily, the bagels started burning, setting off the smoke alarm. In the ensuing dish cloth flapping and window opening, I was able to change the subject to Sam's kidnapping case. I didn't learn much. It seemed Sam was not inclined to talk either.

As soon as he left, Doris was at my door. "I looked at them books last night and there's definitely something wrong. As far as I can tell, they've been underestimating revenues and overestimating expenses. Was there a lot of new furniture and equipment in the office?"

"No, in fact I didn't see anything new."

Doris shook her head. "I don't know how they thought they'd get away with it—a child could figure out what they did."

"Which was?"

"I've got to spend more time on them but basically they owe you almost half as much again as you received this past year. They've reported the right amount of income in the first—correct—set of books and under reported revenues by almost half in the second. Looks as if they got estimates for new furniture and office equipment, never bought anything, but claimed it as a business expense."

"So you're saying that they've cheated me out of almost half my proceeds and they'll file a false business return at the end of the fiscal year which they expect me to sign?"

"That's right."

I had underestimated Doris. I sometimes forgot that she had kept the books for the farm she and her late husband ran together.

"What are you going to do about it, Kate?"

I thought for a moment. "Nothing for now. Let's wait until they ask me to sign the tax return. I'll send copies of both sets of books to Robert Armstrong. He's taken care of our financial affairs for the last thirty years. He should know exactly what Jack and Andrew have done."

"So who was that other woman with you last night? What was her part in all this?"

"She's Jack's secretary and she's the one who told me Jack had two sets of books and that Andrew was his new accountant." I smiled at her. "Andrew's cutting off all financial support and threatening Ellie with loss of custody of the twins. I want him to think he's won and that she's helpless. Then, when he least expects it, we'll strike. He won't know what hit him."

Chapter 31

Doris had to leave. She had—as she phrased it—company arriving.

"We're doing an AAR.

"A what?"

"After Action Review. We do one after all our ops. You know, talk about how it went."

I had no sooner started to clean up the breakfast mess when there was another knock at my door. I hurried to open it, but it wasn't Doris returning. Instead, Sam's daughter, Mira stood there.

"Kate." She gave me a big hug. "I'm in Shelbyville this weekend, but Dad and Kevin are at the precinct. Doris is in some kind of confidential meeting, so I came up to see you and she'll be here as soon as everyone leaves."

She sat down on the couch. "Mom and I are finalizing the wedding plans. We just mailed the invitations, chose the reception menu and decided on the flowers."

Mira and her mother had picked out the venue, a winery on I-74. I'd never visited it, but according to Mira, it had a beautiful reception room and a lovely stone building where the ceremony would be held. Neither Kevin nor Mira wanted a church wedding. At first, both families were upset, but finally accepted their decision.

"Mom wanted a Thanksgiving theme, but we eventually decided on purple and lilac as our colors—very appropriate for a winery. Since you will be sitting in the front row with Dad, Mom and I thought you would like to coordinate outfits."

I was horrified. "Mira, the front row is just for family. Why don't I sit with Doris and Martha?"

She laughed. "It was Dad's idea and Mom is fine with it. After all, my step-father will be in the front row as well. I talked with Ellie and she agreed to let the twins be ring bearers for the ceremony. I know you'll want to be in front, so you can see everything."

Her cell pinged with a text, "Great, Kevin has managed to break free." She gave me another hug. "I'm so excited—just six more weeks."

As she left, I heard the chatter of voices in the front hall as Doris' company departed. A few minutes later, she entered through the front door with Digger trailing after her. He always joined Doris' coffee mornings— there were usually crumbs under the table for him to clean up.

"Kate, did Mira fill you in on all her wedding plans? We'll have to go shopping for our new outfits."

My answer was decidedly unenthusiastic.

"What's wrong?"

I sighed. "Mira wants me to sit in the front row with Sam and his ex-wife."

"Well, what's wrong with that? Mira's step-dad will be there too."

"But I'm not her step anything! I'd rather sit with you and Martha."

Doris laughed. "Don't be silly. You know Sam wants you there. Besides, the twins are going to be ring-bearers. Won't it be cute to see them little ones walking down the aisle? Oh, it's going to be a beautiful wedding. If Mira's mom wears purple, then you can wear lilac or the other way around. Whatever you choose will look lovely."

No support there. Doris was enamored of a fancy wedding with me in the forefront. I listened to her prattling away until she finally changed the subject.

"Kate, Vincent says he will only stay until your foot is healed and you can drive again. How much longer do you think it will be?"

As Doris well knew, my ankle was healed and I was already driving short distances, we just hadn't told Vincent yet. The appointment with the doctor would make it official, something she wanted to delay.

"I have an appointment with the orthopedic surgeon in a couple of weeks and I'm pretty sure the boot will be off and I'll be back to normal."

"Hmmm, that soon..." She nervously tapped her finger on her bottom lip. "I don't want Vincent to go back to sleeping in the school basement, but he's too proud to take any help. Can you think of anything, Kate?"

"Not right now. What did you have in mind?"

"I've got to find him a job so he can stay here. If you hear of anything..."

"You'll be the first to know."

She looked worried so I changed the subject. "How was your AAR?"

"It went well, but Henry thinks it was too much of a close call. He thinks we should have done a better job of planning for contingencies—that's unexpected things that come up."

"Like Jack returning to the scene of the crime."

"Right, but Bob Oppenheim did good with delaying him."

"As did you, Doris."

She gave a satisfied grin. "Yeah, it was fun. That Jack didn't suspect a thing."

"Though it was a close call when he came back the second time. Who was the man who opened the door and dragged us out? And how did he know we needed help?"

"When we saw Jack returning, Bob texted Henry—he's faster than me."

And, no doubt, more legible, but I didn't tell Doris that.

"And since Henry did what he calls his due diligence, he knew the layout of the office and which door on the alley was Jack's."

"Wait a minute, you mean that was Henry?"

She gave me a big grin. "Yep, pretty good, huh?"

So the heavy-set, red faced, homeless man was the frail, feeble Henry. Talk about a master of disguise! He certainly had me fooled.

Chapter 32

After Doris left, I sat down on the couch with a soothing cup of tea. I had a lot to think about. First, Mira's wedding. Sam and I had been dating for over a year, if you counted the times we'd broken up with each other. A few months ago, we had talked about moving in together, but I didn't want to move into Sam's apartment and he didn't want to move into mine.

Why did Mira and Sam want me to sit in the front row with her mother and step-father anyway? That was putting our relationship on a more official level than it was. Front rows at weddings were reserved for family and I most certainly didn't qualify.

Then there was the problem of Vincent. Doris didn't want him to leave but eventually he would have to. I couldn't drag out the broken ankle excuse for much longer. I knew she would be devastated, but I couldn't think of a solution.

And what to do about Ellie? Should I tell her about her father and Andrew? I wanted to relieve some of her stress but I didn't want Jack and Andrew to suspect that I knew about their embezzlement scheme—not yet anyway. First, I wanted to talk to Robert Armstrong to understand exactly what they had done and what the legal ramifications were. Ellie's lawyer could then use that as leverage in the divorce.

I was also worried about Sebastian. He had been stupid to allow himself to be manipulated by Barbara Armstrong. But since he was so open and honest himself, he didn't recognize duplicity in other people.

Why did Bitch Barbara want to be involved in something that was turning out to be an utter disaster? Sylvia seemed to think she was deliberately trying to sabotage the play. But why?

What should I tackle first?

My decision was made for me when the front doorbell rang.

"Mom, it's me, Ellie." I buzzed her in.

She looked pale and wan. The dark shadows under her eyes told me that she hadn't been sleeping. Before I could utter a word she blurted out, "I've decided against divorce for now."

"Why, Ellie?"

"I have to think what's best for the boys. I can't take a chance of losing custody and let Andrew's crazy mother be involved in raising them. I'm going to get a part-time job to pay for college and take classes when they're in school then there'll be no question of my neglecting them. It'll take longer but I'll get it done."

"What if I have a better idea?"

"Like what?"

"Let me ask you this. Did you know that your father is one of Andrew's clients?"

"No, when did that happen?"

I debated telling her everything then went ahead and did. Ellie was no longer a child and I needed to trust her judgment.

"Mom, you broke into Dad's office?"

"I had a key," I said defensively, "and as part-owner, I have a perfect right to examine the books."

A huge grin broke across her face. "Are you telling me that Dad, with Andrew's help, is cooking the books?"

"Yes, I have copies of both sets. I also have your missing financial information and Andrew does have a safety deposit box which I'm sure your lawyer can subpoena."

She gave me a big hug. "You are amazing."

"Ellie, nobody must know about this. I'm giving copies to Robert Armstrong so he can figure out exactly what they have done. We are going to lay low, let your father and Andrew think they have won, then let them find out they haven't."

"How did you figure this out?"

"I had a tip from someone."

She stopped. "Mom, this is sad. How could Dad be so stupid? He could lose his license over this, as could Andrew."

"I'm still trying to figure out why he did it. For the short time they were married, his divorce from Tiffany couldn't have been that costly and business is up for the year."

Tiffany was Jack's former secretary, or personal assistant, as she liked to be called. I called her the blond bimbo. Their affair broke up my 'perfect marriage' and, after our divorce, Jack was stupid enough to marry her, a decision he came to regret.

"Oh, Mom! Ellie was ecstatic. "Do you think it will work?"

"Absolutely, but don't look too happy when you get home. Remember, Andrew thinks he's won and is punishing you."

"I'll be the saddest, happy person you ever saw. Thank you, thank you, thank you."

She embraced me and almost danced down the stairs, only stopping to hug Doris, who was coming up.

Doris looked surprised. "Ellie seems happy."

"I told her about the cooked books. She'd almost decided she had no choice but to stay with Andrew."

I saw Doris open her mouth to admonish me, so I quickly interjected, "She'll work on her sad face on the way home."

"I'm still looking for a job for Vincent. I wanted to ask you about Charlie's trust. What if the trust paid tuition and board at IU Bloomington? You're one of the trustees, do you think that's a good use of our money?"

"I think that would be an excellent use. Let's meet with Enid and Rose to talk about it."

Doris beamed. "And Vincent can still stay with me during the holidays."

Chapter 33

Sam called and asked me to meet him for lunch at the deli on the Square. When I got there he was sitting at our favorite table in the back.

After I took the chair opposite him he said, "Has Mira talked to you about the wedding? We'll be sitting in the front row with my ex-wife and her husband."

"Sam, that makes me..." I hesitated, "uncomfortable."

I saw his jaw clench. "Why uncomfortable? Are you saying you'd prefer to sit with someone else?"

I didn't answer right away and he turned away from me. "Sorry, I misread that one—won't happen again."

He called the waitress over. "Can I have my order to go?"

"Sam, don't be childish. Next you'll be asking me not to come to the wedding."

He bit back his answer and walked over to the counter to pick up his food. As he made his way to the door, I saw him stop, take a deep breath then he walked back to the table.

"I'm sorry, Kate, that was stupid of me. I've had a lot on my mind with this case, but it's no excuse."

I had a lot on my mind too, but it didn't give me leave to act like a complete ass. "You're not the only one with problems, Sam. Ellie has filed for divorce. Her husband is fighting for custody of the children. He's hidden all the assets of the marriage so she has no money. My ex-husband is cheating me out of revenue from the law office. He also refuses to help Ellie. In fact he's supporting Andrew. Sebastian's play is turning out to be a complete disaster and Doris is upset because Vincent will be moving out in a couple of weeks. So excuse me if I can't dredge up much sympathy because your feelings are hurt over me not wanting to sit in the front row at Mira's wedding."

He opened his mouth to speak, decided against it, picked up his food package and left.

I sat back in my chair. Why did relationships have to be so difficult? Why couldn't Sam accept that we weren't to that point yet? Would it have been better to lie to him and say I'd love to sit in the parents' row? Women were always expected to be the ones to make all the concession, to nurture. Right now I needed to be nurtured.

Martha came through the door and made her way over to me. "What's up with Sam? He looks as if he could spit nails. So do you for that matter."

I didn't want to get into my problems with Martha. She would always take Sam's side. Instead I said, "Ellie wants a divorce and her husband is being difficult. He's playing games with their finances and it's going to be tough for all of us."

"Are the twins still going to be ring bearers?"

"As far as I know."

"And Sam wants you to sit in the same row as his ex-wife and her husband."

So Sam had told her.

I shrugged my shoulders.

Martha shook her head. "You don't want to and Sam got bent out of shape, right?"

The waitress came over. "Can I take your order now?"

I didn't want to discuss the bridal seating arrangements or Sam's hurt feelings any longer, so I said, "No, I have to leave."

Instead of going back home, I went to the restaurant near the hospital, ordered a huge corned beef sandwich with fries and ate all of it.

On my way out the door, comfortably replete, I stood aside for a couple entering. They passed me without a second glance and I was about to descend the front steps when it occurred to me that one half of the duo looked familiar. I decided to check it out so re-entered the restaurant.

They were seated next to the window. I took a center table behind them where I could see what was going on. The expensively-dressed older woman, with the fistful of sparkling rings, had her back to me, but the man glanced my way without the slightest sign of recognition. It was Henry but a very different Henry from the last time I had seen him.

His hair was silver gray and on the long side. He was wearing a beautifully cut suit that almost matched his hair. With the ornate silver and ruby signet ring that graced his left hand and the dark red and silver ascot with matching ruby stick pin, he was a perfectly coordinated and very handsome, albeit older, man about town. By the way the woman was giggling at almost everything he said and leaning across the table to squeeze his hand, she agreed with my assessment.

I ordered a small salad that I didn't need from the server, who was surprised to see me again, and tried to unobtrusively eavesdrop on their conversation. It was hard to glean anything from the tete-a-tete. Everything Henry said was drowned out by the squeals and giggles of his totally enthralled table companion. The only thing I was able to gather was that Henry now seemed to be named Darnley and my ears pricked up when he mentioned *The Heiress.*

"One of my favorite plays, my beloved Winona," he said loftily.

The giggler blushed. "Have you've played the father before?"

"Dear lady, it was my most successful role of the season. I'll have to dig out my reviews for your edification."

There was more giggling. 'Darnley' leaned across the table and spoke softly to her. I picked away at my salad and tried to look as if I were not hanging on their every word.

She playfully slapped his arm. "You're terrible."

He took her hand and brought it to his lips. "Only when I'm with you."

There was more whispering and laughter then Winona leaned across the table. "I would so love you to play him for me. Please say you will?"

He pushed up a highly starched cuff to glance at his watch, which, from where I was sitting, looked remarkably like a Rolex. "Winona, my dear, delightful though this has been, I have another appointment. We must do this again and discuss it."

A gushing Winona scrambled to her feet and Darnley offered her his arm. As they passed my table he glanced at me, one eyelid discreetly closed, and he and the still prattling Winona, exited together.

So Winona wanted 'Darnley' to play the father for her in *The Heiress?* How did she plan to accomplish that since Sebastian was the director? I couldn't wait to get back to the house to pass on the information to Doris, Clarice and the rest of the crew.

Chapter 34

The first thing I did after arriving home was to call Doris. "You'll never guess what I heard today."

"Oh, yes, I will," was her answer. "Come on down."

I flew down the stairs and into Doris' apartment. As I came in the front, Enid and Rose, with Digger at their heels, came in the back door through the kitchen. Both were wearing their work clothes and hadn't even taken time to clean the paint from their hands. Digger did his little dance as soon as he saw me but started to bark as someone rang the door bell.

It was Henry, but a very different Henry from the one that had left the restaurant. It seemed he was not only a master of disguise, but a quick change artist as well. If I had passed this Henry on the street and someone asked what he looked like, I would have been hard pressed to answer. The handsome charming actor, who winked at me as he left the restaurant, had morphed into a bland, nondescript creature, the type that was instantly forgotten. I tried to analyze how he could effect such a change with only a few minor details in dress but couldn't. It was an alteration in demeanor—something internal—as if he'd thrown a switch and become someone else.

Doris bustled into the kitchen for coffee and cake while Henry fetched a chair and placed it next to a small table. As soon as he was comfortably settled he took a sip of coffee then stood, surveying the room.

Clarice, who had sat quietly until now, gave an exasperated snort. "Don't keep us in suspense, Henry. Did you or did you not find out what is going on?"

"I did," he replied.

"Well, tell us," she snapped. "We don't have all day."

He smiled. "First, Clarice, why don't you explain your part in all this?"

Clarice was brief, "I've known Barbara Armstrong since grade school. I also know she has absolutely no interest in theater. So I joined the group and became her best friend to find out her agenda."

"Which was?" Doris was on the edge of her seat.

"She wouldn't tell me directly, just dropped a lot of hints about how Sebastian was going to be kicked out very shortly and that the theater board was going to replace him with someone better. I started following her and, a couple of weeks ago, saw her with some woman that I've never seen before. I heard her mention the play, but when she saw me the conversation immediately ceased. I asked around and learned the woman was a Mrs. Winona Bradley and that's all I could find out."

Henry took up the narrative. "Clarice asked me to investigate and I learned that Mrs. Winona Bradley has recently moved to Shelbyville from Edinburgh, in Shelby County. From my contacts there, I learned that she is a lover of theater and was frustrated with the local drama society because she was never allowed to direct any of their plays. There was a reason for that. The drama society has high standards and, according to the president, Winona has no talent as a director, actor or singer. Her husband made a large donation to the group which she felt entitled her to a directorial role for one of their musical productions—*The Unsinkable*

Molly Brown. It was a complete fiasco. The donation was returned and a new director chosen."

Clarice checked her watch. "I have to leave soon. What's her connection to Bitch Barbara and our play?"

"She met Barbara Armstrong at the church they both attend and somehow Barbara learned of her interest in directing. Probably, because Winona tells anyone who will listen, that she was the leading light of the Pixy Theater in Edinburgh. The Bradleys are wealthy, influential and love to entertain. Since her divorce, Barbara Armstrong has lost almost all her social circle and a close relationship with Mrs. Bradley will go a long way to reinstate her in the upper echelon of Shelbyville society. She is therefore trying to become Winona's best friend. Barbara has convinced Mrs. Bradley that, under Sebastian's direction, *The Heiress*, will be a total disaster and that she is speaking to the theater board on her behalf and that she, Winona, will step into Sebastian's shoes and direct the play."

Sylvia stood up. "No way is that going to happen. I'm going to contact everyone who has quit and tell them what's happening."

Clarice shook her head. "It's going to take more than that. We have to convince Sebastian that Bitch Barbara is plotting to oust him."

There was an enigmatic smile on Doris' face. "I think I have a plan that will work."

The whole room sat forward but Doris put up her hand to stop the questions.

"Let me work out the details. We'll meet back here in two days."

As the others left, I lingered behind hoping to learn more. But, try as I might, not another word could I get out of her. She merely shook her head and told me, "You'll know when I got it all figured out."

I finally gave up and returned to my own apartment.

Chapter 35

Are you still mad at me?
I texted back, *I don't know.*
Can we talk about it?
Reluctantly I replied, *Guess so.*

I'd barely taken my thumbs off the keyboard when Sam walked into the living room. By then I'd decided I didn't want to talk about the wedding. I had too many other things to worry about.

He was carrying a bottle of my favorite wine. "Can I pour you a glass?"

I nodded, still not in the mood for conversation. He handed me a generous portion, poured one for himself and sat down next to me on the couch.

We sipped our wine in silence until Sam finally spoke, "You still don't want to talk about today?"

"You're the detective—what do you think?"

He topped off my glass and his own. "What if I tell you what's happening with the case?"

"Sure."

He exhaled a deep breath. "We think Ted Thompson is involved though we can't prove it yet. He and Dr. Cutler seem to be close friends and spend a lot of time together."

"But Dr. Cutler doesn't drive."

"He used to. Up until last summer he had a current driver's license which he didn't renew. There is no car registered to him, but the administrative assistant, who picks him up from school occasionally, drives a car which used to belong to him."

"Is she involved?"

"Nothing points to her as yet, but the tech team going over the Quonset hut found a lot of physical evidence—hair, fibers, fingerprints and DNA. As soon as it's processed, we'll be able to get somewhere."

He shook his head. "That's enough about the case. Kate, can we talk about today? I know I was a complete ass."

There seemed no way to avoid it. "Yes, you were, and if we start arguing I want you to leave immediately."

"Agreed."

He waited and then, when he realized I wasn't going to say anything more, said, "I know we never talk about—you know—us, but it doesn't mean I don't think about it a lot."

I didn't answer and he seemed to lose the thread of his conversation. After some hemming and hawing all he could come up with was to ask me if I wanted more wine.

I raised my almost full glass. "I haven't finished this yet."

"Oh, yes." He cleared his throat and took another stab at it. "What I'm trying to say is that I only want to date you and I've felt that way since we met. I'm hoping you feel the same way—you know, exclusive."

For Sam that was a huge announcement.

I waited until he went on, "I thought us sitting together at the wedding would sort of let everyone know that we—it—was serious that we—you know." He stopped, red-faced. "Kate, you do feel the same way, don't you, about being exclusive?"

"Of course I do, you idiot, but it doesn't mean I'm ready to announce it to the whole world."

"But we are exclusive now?"

"We are."

The best thing about fighting with Sam was making up with Sam. The next morning as we were lazing over breakfast, he said, "Now we're okay, can I ask about your secret mission with Doris?"

I hesitated.

He hurriedly said, "It's all right if you'd rather not. It's just that, if I don't know, I worry about—umm—what you're doing. When you and Doris get together you're sometimes… reckless."

"I wouldn't call it reckless, Sam. We accomplished what we set out to do and nobody got hurt—yet…" I said thinking of Jack and Andrew's shock when I confront them with their payment scam.

His eyes were locked on mine and didn't waver. I took a deep breath, "I heard from an anonymous source—well, not anonymous to me—that my ex-husband has been cheating me out of about half my income from the business by keeping two sets of books. As part owner, I still have a key to the office so I let myself in after hours and made copies of both sets."

"And Doris came with you?"

"The only people who entered the office had a right to be there. Doris was merely the lookout. She does whatever she wants," I quickly told him as he started to speak.

Sam grinned at me. "So the anonymous source was your husband's secretary and she was the second person in the office."

"How did you know?"

He laughed. "As you so often tell me, I'm the detective. What else happened?"

"Jack came back and almost caught us, but we got out in time and I have all the information that I need."

His phone pinged. He glanced down at the screen then lifted me off my feet in a crushing embrace. "Gotta go. Can I see you tonight?"

The enthusiastic farewell I gave him seemed to be the answer he wanted.

Chapter 36

"Kate, I have my plan ready."

Doris had been lying in wait for me and, as I came down the back stairs on my way to work the morning shift at the library, she pounced.

"Can we meet at my place tonight?"

"Sure, who else will be coming?"

"As many as I can get—keep it quiet though; I don't want that woman to get a hint of what we're doing."

By 'that woman' I knew she was referring to Bitch Barbara. I couldn't wait to hear her plan.

It seemed I wasn't the only one who felt that way. As I passed the librarian's desk, Sylvia stopped me. "Do you know what Doris is up to?"

"No, just that she has a secret plan."

She laughed. "For ridding us of...?"

Sebastian walked towards us. I hurriedly left for the back room where Clarice grabbed my arm in an iron grip. "You'll be there tonight, right?"

"I wouldn't miss it for the world."

The morning went by slowly for all of us.

Doris had asked us to be at her place by five. At ten minutes till, I looked out my front window to see the street lined with cars. There was a lot of noise coming from downstairs and I hurried down so as to not miss anything.

The apartment was crowded. There were even people sitting on the floor—it looked as if the whole theater was there.

First, Doris introduced Henry. Since only a few of the group knew who he was, there was a lot of interest when he started talking.

He was back to the erudite actor persona. "Doris and some of her friends asked me to find out why Barbara Armstrong had inserted herself into Sebastian's play when up until now she has never shown the slightest interest in theater."

Stephen spoke up. "What did you discover? I'm not the only one who feels that she is deliberately sabotaging the play. I told Sebastian, but he refused to listen."

"That's exactly what she's doing." Henry looked around the room. He certainly had everyone's attention. "Now you probably want to know why."

"Well, yes," spat out Clarice. "She's a very spiteful woman, but there's usually a reason for her actions."

"Barbara was recently divorced."

"And Sebastian feels sorry for her. We already know that," she sniffed.

Henry smiled. "Clarice, you became her best friend. Why don't you tell the group what you learned?"

"As Bitch Barbara's best friend, I became privy to a lot of her secrets, including her little acts of sabotage, such as hiding the props and interfering with sound cues. We giggled over that a lot."

There was an anguished squeal from Cindy who was sitting on the floor in front of the couch and a roar of anger from the back of the room, "I knew someone had messed with my tape. Sebastian didn't believe me. When I see that woman..."

"Be quiet, Ron. Let me finish."

Ron subsided into a low rumble and Clarice continued, "She told me that the play was going to be a disaster, one of her favorite words, and would need a new director. I agreed with her and tried to find out what she had in mind, but she just gave me one of her stupid giggles and told me I'd learn soon enough. I saw her in Luigi's bar having a drink with two of the theater board members and later with Winona Bradley."

She looked for Henry to take over and he stood up again. "I did a little investigating in Edinburgh and found that in spite of her husband's making a very munificent donation to the theater, the board returned the donation and said goodbye to Mrs. Bradley."

"Tell them why, Henry," Clarice demanded.

"Because her self-image exceeded her talent—which was nonexistent. When they relocated to Shelbyville, she met Barbara at the church they both attend. Since her divorce, Mrs. Armstrong has become somewhat of a pariah and she saw Winona as her entrée into a new social circle."

There wasn't a sound in the room. Henry continued, "Barbara has virtually promised Winona that she can oust Sebastian and take over *The Heiress* as director. The meeting with the theater board members was her first step to convince them that the production will be a total flop. That's why she's been actively getting rid of any of Sebastian's supporters. She plans on bringing the board members and Winona to the next rehearsal, where no doubt, she will have a few disruptive acts arranged."

He looked around at the enthralled faces hanging on his every word. "Mrs. Bradley thinks I'm a performer and has offered me the part of Dr. Sloper since she's been told the actor playing that role has quit."

There was a horrified gasp from the entire room which included the erstwhile Dr. Sloper who had been persuaded to return to the cast.

Doris piped up, "But I have a plan and we have to work together. I want all of us who quit, or didn't want to be in the play because of that woman, to contact

Sebastian and beg to be re-admitted to the show. Let me tell you some of the things we're going to do."

Stephen and I ran upstairs to my apartment to fetch the bottles of champagne I had on ice and together the whole cast and crew toasted to the downfall of Barbara Armstrong and her protégé.

Chapter 37

I'm not a forgiving person and it was hard to appear contrite when Sebastian was the one who was at fault. My apology wasn't nearly as heartfelt as Doris' who had refused to work on the costumes more as a show of solidarity with me than because of any deep seated-anger towards Sebastian. She was happy to be back in the fold.

I muttered a feeble, "I guess if you need me, I'll come back in spite of our differences." The relief on Sebastian's face was as touching as the bear hug he bestowed on me. He walked around the library with a beaming smile on his face for the rest of the day.

My act of contrition was worth any embarrassment I might have felt when I saw the stunned look on Bitch Barbara's face when Doris and I walked into rehearsal that evening. My petty triumph was doubled when Cindy, Stephen, Ron and the rest of the cast and crew followed behind.

She quickly turned on Sebastian, "I'm not going to let these people waltz right back in after quitting on you the way they did."

Her face was contorted in anger, a very different look from the simpering sweetness she usually showed him. I could tell he was shocked by the change.

"Barbara, I'm the director. I'll make that decision."

His voice was gentle, but I could sense the steel underlying his tone of voice. Barbara heard it too and hastily backtracked. "Of course, you are, Sebastian. I'm just looking out for you. I don't want them to leave you in the lurch again."

The cast and crew ignored her and crowded around Sebastian. To Barbara's vexation, Cindy plopped down in the chair next to him while Stephen went backstage to rustle up a cup of coffee. The Bitch disappeared for a few minutes then came back and took her usual place on Sebastian's other side. I noticed that he didn't seem inclined to listen to whatever she was whispering in his ear. In fact, a couple of times he held up his hand to silence her.

The door at the back of the auditorium opened and Winona Bradley entered with two men I didn't recognize. They took a seat near the front of the theater and a few minutes later Actor Henry joined them, stick pin and all.

Sebastian had his back to them but by the pleased smirk that crossed the Bitch's face it was obvious they were expected.

She gave them a little hand wave. "We have an audience tonight," she gushed. "Why don't we start at the beginning of Act One?"

Sebastian looked irritated. He leaned over and whispered in her ear.

Barbara put her hand up to her mouth to cover her giggle. "I'm sorry, Sebastian. I didn't mean to step on your toes. It's just that we have so many cast openings…"

She leaned around and spoke to the group sitting behind Sebastian, "We've had a hard time with casting the play and a lot of the actors have quit. Poor Sebastian is at his wits end."

Poor Sebastian was beginning to lose his temper. He barked out, "Ron, can we have the opening music. I want to cut it a little."

The music started and the smirk on Barbara's face slowly faded. The opening went without a hitch until Stephen dashed onstage. He was carrying a decanter. Shielding his eyes from the glare of the stage lights, he peered out into the auditorium. "Cindy, isn't this supposed to be onstage?"

Cindy's squeaky little voice answered him, "What are you doing with that? I already set it on the side table."

"Barbara Armstrong moved it. I want to know why." He glared at Barbara. "Props are Cindy's responsibility, not yours."

Barbara almost stuttered, "I didn't move it, you must be mistaken."

"It was no mistake. I saw you take it from the table and put it back in the prop room on the shelf. Did you forget it's used in Act One? You also replaced Ron's music tape with another. Luckily, when I pointed it out to him, he used the backup tape he'd made for just such a contingency."

Barbara flushed an unbecoming shade of puce. "Sebastian, I don't know what he's talking…"

Sebastian cut her off, "We'll discuss this later. Let's get on with rehearsal."

With a meaningful look at the unknown men, sitting in the auditorium, she said, "Did you forget we don't have a maid? She quit."

Doris stepped forward. "Since you're not production staff, you wouldn't know that part's already been recast. I'm playing Maria."

Barbara almost collapsed in her chair.

Under Sebastian's direction, Doris went through the opening of the play where the maid lights the oil lamps. The light cues went off without a hitch.

The actor playing Dr. Sloper appeared onstage. Doris delivered her first line, "Good evening, Doctor."

He crossed to a small desk and placed his medical bag upon it. Before Doris could even open her mouth to utter her next line, there was an anguished howl from the auditorium.

A furious Henry/Darnley turned to Winona, "Why is that man playing the role you promised me? How could you do this to me?" He staggered out into the aisle, "Winona, I trusted you."

A distraught Winona tried to placate him, "Barbara told me he had quit and the role was going to be yours as soon as the theater board fired the incompetent who's in charge now. I'm going to be the new director."

Barbara knew the actor had quit. Clarice and cast neglected to tell her that he had been reinstated.

A thundering voice declaimed, "I demand that I be allowed to audition."

Without waiting for an answer, Darnley rushed down the aisle, leapt upon the stage, took center and stood for a moment, head down breathing heavily

A stunned Sebastian was rooted to the spot in disbelief.

Raising his head and looking up to the balcony, Darnley began a highly charged emotional monologue, the point in the first act where Dr. Sloper explains why he dislikes his daughter.

He was absolutely abysmal. He paced, gyrated, dropped his voice to a whisper then roared at the bewildered crowd. The board members hid their faces in embarrassment. Even the infatuated Winona turned away from his over-the-top rendition.

It was when Darnley almost screamed, "What would you like me to do for her?" that Sebastian pulled himself together and ended the painful performance.

"I'm sorry Mr. Whomever you are. I'm afraid you've been misled. Auditions are closed. The role is already cast and I am the director, not Mrs. Bradley. I suggest you leave."

Darnley staggered from the stage, leaned over the orchestra pit and, with a fist pressed to his forehead, declaimed, "Winona, you have betrayed me. I will never forgive you for this." He stumbled up the aisle, turned and with a grief-stricken, "Farewell," exited.

Winona collapsed in a flood of tears. The board members who had expected a totally different outcome were trying to fade away up the aisle before they were identified. Sebastian turned to a quivering Barbara Armstrong.

He was only able to spit out two words, but they were imbued with an anger so fierce two were all that were needed. "GET OUT."

The Bitch picked up her purse and almost ran out of the auditorium, with a sobbing Winona Bradley at her heels.

Sebastian buried his face in his hands. It took him a few moments to recover. Finally, he raised his head and wiping away his tears said, "I should have listened to you. You were right and I was too stupid and egotistical to see it. I apologize to everyone. I wouldn't blame you if you walked out right now, but I hope you'll stay."

There was a murmur of support from the assembled actors and crew. Doris stood up. "What's done is done and there's no use crying over spilt milk. Like they say in the movies—we've got a show to do."

The whole theater applauded and we started rehearsal from the top.

Chapter 38

My life was gradually falling back into place. Even though I had yet to get clearance from the orthopedic surgeon, I had discarded the boot and soon would be able to wear something other than, what Doris called, sensible shoes. Maybe even something frivolous.

Robert Armstrong had received the purloined books. Knowing how conscientious he was, it would probably take him at least a couple of weeks to verify all the information. He was saddened by the news that Jack was attempting to embezzle from the business.

"Kate, he did ask me one time if there was some way to reduce the quarterly payments you receive. I told him no, but had no idea he would do something that was not only unethical but also illegal. My advice is to not sign the annual tax forms until I've seen them. Can you get copies for me?"

"I'll tell him that my accountant insists that he check any financial forms before I sign. He'll have no choice in the matter."

Poor Robert, he and Jack had been friends for almost thirty years. It was difficult for him to accept that a man he once admired could sink so low.

In the meantime, I needed new shoes, or rather, I *wanted* new shoes.

"Doris, come shoe shopping with me."

"Are they for the wedding?"

"Possibly."

"Can we stop by the butcher's first? I need to order ground beef and some chickens. We're planning a barbecue at the Senior Center."

"I know," she said in reply to my raised eyebrows, "but we love barbecue and the weather's not too cold to cook outside right now, so why not?"

I was in no hurry, so agreed. Shoe shopping tended to be a lengthy affair and we set out early. I parked near the butcher's and, as we were walking along the sidewalk, Doris grabbed my arm, "Look. No. There!" She pointed toward the shop. Prominent among the display of dismembered animals in the front window was a sign 'Help Wanted.' Doris almost sprinted towards the door.

She burst in, "Bertram, did you get any applications?"

The butcher, Bertram Fletcher, was perplexed, "For what?"

"For the job," Doris answered.

"Not anyone I want to hire."

"I have the perfect person for you. He's a college student and a real hard worker. Right now he drives Kate and me around."

Bertram looked puzzled as well he might, since I was obviously capable of driving myself.

I explained. "My broken ankle is about healed, and now that I can drive, Vincent will be looking for another job."

"Well…" Doris looked at him pleadingly. There were tears in her eyes. The butcher came out from behind the counter to give her a big hug. She was almost lost in his massive arms.

Patting his back, which she could barely reach, she looked up in his face. "Are you doing better now? How are you managing?"

"It's hard without Ada. I'm thinking of selling the farm to concentrate on the shop."

Bertram Fletcher's wife, Ada, was in a mental institution. After the death of their only child, she'd had a complete breakdown. It was doubtful she would ever be released.

Doris looked shocked. "But you love the farm, Bertram. It's been in your family for generations."

He shook his head sadly. "I know."

"Anyway, I can help with your job opening." She quickly described Vincent. "You want I should have him stop by to talk to you."

"Yes. But I can't pay top wages here, Doris. With the farm to manage, business is down, because, without Ada, I'm only open three days a week. There's a furnished apartment over the shop he can have for free."

"I'll call him right now and send him over."

In her excitement, she almost forgot to place her order for the Senior Center, but with farewell hugs for Bertram and a further glowing endorsement of Vincent, we finally managed to break away and head for the shoe store.

Walking back to the car, Doris was ecstatic, "He'll be perfect for Bertram and he'll still be living close by so we can keep an eye on him."

After trying on about thirty pairs of shoes, I pared it down to a final three. I couldn't choose between them so decided to take them all. Doris wasn't ready to leave. She kept finding shoes for the wedding—especially purple and lilac shoes.

"Look at these with the little straps. They'd be perfect."

They would, if I were sitting in the front row and wearing a purple or lilac outfit which I wasn't going to be. After every single pair she found for me to try on either didn't fit properly, had heels that were too high, pinched my toes or hurt my arches, she eventually accepted that I would be buying no lilac or purple wedding shoes that day.

Chapter 39

Though Digger had many admirable qualities, I would be the first to admit that he was not a well trained dog. He walked reasonably well on the leash but was liable to take off after any chattering squirrel or bounding rabbit, pulling me along with him and he never came when called. I was walking him on the high school running track, one of our favorite places because it bordered a wooded slope where, with his nose crisscrossing the ground, he loved to follow animal scents. I was distracted by a text from Doris who was determined to find the purple or lilac wedding shoes she still thought I needed.

I justfound someshoos youll lik ina catalog willshowyou when home

While I was trying to decipher Doris' message and control Digger, a crow swooped down low over the grass in front of him and, with an excited bark, he jerked the leash from my hand and took off after it.

"Digger, get back here!"

He ignored me and was soon out of sight. I ran in the direction he had gone, but he'd disappeared.

Panic set in. Once he started chasing something, he rarely gave up. I ran towards the wooded area at the side of the running track, but eventually had to stop. I leaned against a tree, out of breath and panting, surveying the area. Even if I spotted him, I wouldn't have had the energy to take up the chase again. But he was nowhere in sight. My ankle started to throb and I stumbled towards a bench at the bottom of a shallow hill. I had just collapsed onto its sturdy seat when I heard a yip. Coming over the hill was Digger. He was on the leash and being led by Henry.

As soon as he saw me, he sprinted down the hill with a joyful bark but the frail Henry had no problem keeping up with him and arrived at my seat barely winded.

"Mrs. Conley, here's your errant hound. May I join you?"

I nodded and he took a seat after carefully securing Digger to the back of the bench. I decided he was Nonentity Henry today, rather than Frail Henry.

"How's the play going?"

"Very well," I said. "Doris and I are both enjoying it."

We were. I loved the role of *Elizabeth Almond* and Doris was thrilled to be 'treading the boards' as she phrased it, as the family maid. The best part was working with old friends again. I hadn't realized how much I missed our theater group.

"Have you decided on your classes for the next semester of college?"

"I'm planning on taking two history and two anthropology classes."

"And you and the police detective are getting along well?

"Yes."

I was beginning to wonder where he was going with all his questions. This seemed more along the lines of an interrogation than a conversation.

"But he hasn't found the person who is kidnapping students from IUPUI?"

"Not yet," I replied, a little defensively. Sam was still waiting on the forensics. It could be up to six weeks or more before all the material was processed.

His job would be a lot easier if he could get immediate results like the television shows Doris loved to watch.

"Altogether five students have been kidnapped and you were almost one of the victims. I was told Vincent saved you."

This had gone far enough. "Henry, I don't feel comfortable discussing this with you. Detective Williamson doesn't want me talking about the case."

He laughed. "Fair enough. Do you want to discuss why you had to break into your ex-husband's law office instead?"

"I didn't break in. I had a key."

"But you still didn't want him to know you'd been there."

"That's hardly your concern."

"Cheating you out of your fair share of the profits, was he? I don't blame you for being angry." His face had an almost mocking expression.

"Did Doris tell you that?"

"Doris only told me that you needed to get some paperwork."

He stood. "Are you rested enough? We could take Digger for a turn around the running track."

I wanted to get away from Henry. "I think I'd better be getting back to my house."

"I'll walk with you."

I stopped and confronted him, "Who are you, Henry, and what do you want with me?"

He shrugged his shoulders. "I'm just an old man with too much time on his hands who used to work in a boring low level security job, basically counting widgets, and now has fantasies about being a detective. Doris asked some of us at the Senior Center to help with a stalking situation involving you and your daughter. It didn't take me long to find out that, rather than being stalked, you had previously been drugged and almost kidnapped. I've been keeping a close eye on you ever since."

"So you counted widgets? And for that you became a master of disguise and a man of many parts?"

He shrugged. "Theater's always been a passion of mine. I would have joined the company except that playing the debonair Henry was too much fun to pass up. Admit it. You loved seeing Bitch Barbara get her comeuppance."

I did but I wasn't going to acknowledge that to Henry.

He checked his watch, which was a Timex this time rather than a Rolex—Henry was nothing if not detail-oriented. "Mrs. Conley. Let me at least walk you to the front of the school."

We finally parted ways and I was left wondering how Henry knew that five girls had been kidnapped when one of them had never been reported to the media.

Chapter 40

"Kate, Kate."

Doris came rushing out of her kitchen door the moment Digger and I set foot on the back stairs.

"Come on in. I have good news for you.'

There was no tea or cake ready for me. Doris was too excited to bother with small details—whatever she wanted to share couldn't wait.

"It's Vincent. Bertram gave him the job."

"Bertram hired him on the spot?"

"Not only hired him, gave him the apartment over the shop as part of his benefits." Doris was beaming. "That means he'll be staying in Shelbyville and still going to IUPUI. He's going to learn all about the trade—it'll be good for both of them. Bertram's been real lonely since his son died and his wife's been in the mental hospital."

"I ran into Henry when I was walking Digger at the high school track and we had a very interesting talk. He knows all about the student kidnappings, the fact that I copied the account books at Jack's office and his cheating me out of money."

Doris was horrified. "I swear, Kate. I didn't tell him any of that."

"No, I don't believe you did, so how did he find out?"

She answered me carefully, "I like Henry and what we've been doing is a lot of fun, but I sense there's more to him than he's letting on."

"Do you think he's some kind of spy?"

"I don't know what to think. Whatever it is, it's more than helping us with our problems. Some days I think he's a lonely old man with nothing better to do but…"

"At other times he's asking questions about unrelated things that he should know nothing about."

"Yes."

"Maybe we should be investigating Henry?"

"Maybe."

"Doris, why don't we eat out tonight?"

I had returned to my apartment, looked in the refrigerator, found nothing I wanted to eat, and decided I was in the mood for Italian food that included tiramisu for dessert. There was only one place to go—my favorite restaurant, Luigi's. I was hoping Doris would go with me since I had heard nothing from Sam.

Luckily, Doris didn't feel like cooking either and agreed that Luigi's was the perfect choice.

It was still early, so the restaurant wasn't crowded and we were seated in the main dining room against the far wall, the perfect location for people watching. We ordered wine. Doris rarely touched alcohol but dining at Luigi's was a special treat for her and she decided to indulge in a glass of dessert wine, not liking what she called those 'bitter tasting ones.'

As we relaxed over our wine, a man passed by our table. He glanced our way with a look of complete indifference on his face. It was Nonentity Henry. I doubted that anyone else in the room even noticed him.

I kicked Doris under the table.

"Ow…I seen him," she whispered.

We watched him take a table opposite ours.

We were halfway through our entrees when we discovered the reason for Henry's restaurant visit. It certainly wasn't to taste Luigi's excellent food. He ordered a bottle of wine and a small appetizer that he hardly touched.

I immediately recognized the man who stood in the entrance scanning the dining room. He was the professor who taught Greek history at IUPUI. I struggled to remember his name—Fleming—that was it—Arthur Fleming. I had been introduced to him in the break room at IUPUI by Dr. Cutler, the medieval history teacher.

Dr. Fleming had evidently located the person he had come to see—Henry. They greeted each other like old friends, ordered dinner and engaged in an intense conversation. We were too far away to hear what was said and neither of us was any kind of expert in lip reading so we had to deduce what we could from their body language. It wasn't much.

Doris and I ordered more wine, ate as slowly as we could then called the waiter over and asked for the dessert menu to spin the meal out as long as possible. Just when we were about to give up, pay our bill, and leave, Dr. Fleming stood, shook Henry's hand and hurried out of the restaurant. Henry waited a few moments then went after him.

Doris threw down her napkin and followed them out. I paid the bill and tagged along after Doris. I was in time to see an old maroon car exit the parking lot. "Is that Fleming's car?"

"Yes."

A black SUV pulled out behind it. "There's Henry now. I think he's following that teacher." She looked at me. "I wonder why."

I wondered, too.

My car was parked around back and by the time we got to it both Henry and Dr. Fleming were out of sight. That ended our detecting for that evening, but I couldn't wait to share everything with Sam.

Chapter 41

Early the next morning my phone rang. It was Robert Armstrong. "Kate, I've almost finished with the books. Can you get a copy of the tax return for me? I want to see what's been reported as income."

I promised him I would. Jack had left a couple of messages on my voice-mail which I neglected to return. Since we had no communication other than business, he was probably calling about my signing the return.

Robert left me with a warning. "Under no circumstance do I want you to sign anything until I've seen it."

No worries there. I had absolutely no intention of signing the form until Robert had gone over it with a fine tooth comb. Coincidentally, as soon as I hung up from Robert's call, the phone rang again. It was Sarah, Jack's secretary. From the formality of the call, Jack must have been standing near the phone. "Mrs. Conley, Mr. Conley would like you to come into the office to sign the annual tax return. Do you have any time open today?"

Normally, I would have chosen a time at my convenience not Jack's, but I was impatient to get the whole business over with.

We set a time for early afternoon.

When I entered the office, Jack's door was closed and Sarah was sitting behind her desk. In front of her were the tax documents and an already stamped manila envelope. By reading upside down I saw that the tax return had already been signed by Jack, with Andrew's signature affixed as preparer.

Sarah looked over at Jack's door, "He asked me to get you to sign it and then I'm supposed to mail it on my way home."

"Where's my copy?"

She apologetically indicated the papers on her desk. "This is all I have." Then she whispered, "You're not going to sign it, are you?"

"Definitely not. Does he have a client in with him?"

"No, just your son-in-law."

I picked up the sheaf of papers, walked over to the office door and without knocking went in.

Jack and Andrew were leaning over his desk looking at the account books which Andrew immediately covered with Jack's desk blotter. Their shocked faces had guilt written all over.

I smiled sweetly and waved the tax return at them. "I can't sign this until my accountant goes over it."

They looked at each other in consternation. Andrew recovered first. "Actually, we need to mail that today.' He tried to laugh it off. "Don't want to pay any penalties for filing late."

I almost said, "Give me a break". It had been a lot of years but, before we hired Robert, I had done all the bookkeeping and knew that the deadline for filing was at least eight weeks away.

"I'm sure I'll get it back to you in time but if not you can always file for a continuance."

Sweat broke out on Jack's forehead. "Kate, why don't we take care of everything today? Just sign it and we'll be done with the whole business."

I smiled again. "I'm sorry Jack, no can do. Robert made me promise to not sign anything until he had seen it first."

I tucked the papers inside my purse and walked to the door.

Andrew tried to stop me. "You can't take those. They're the only copies we have."

"Andrew, don't be ridiculous. Download another copy."

I turned back. "He'll be contacting you about going over the books."

Jack stuttered, "Why—I mean, Kate, you've never needed to check the books before."

"That was when Robert Armstrong was our accountant. Now he's been replaced, I'd be foolish to take the word of someone new. After all, I have to protect my interests."

As I left, Jack sank back into his chair. Andrew looked decidedly nervous and Sarah gave me a thumbs-up.

Chapter 42

Sarah called me before I reached the house. "I thought you should know. Your son-in-law has forged your signature on the tax forms and they're already mailed."

I was shocked. It seemed a stupid thing to do. "What does he intend to do with the copy I have?"

"I heard them talking. Mr. Conley was panicking and saying they should redo it, but the accountant said that it had worked last year, so there was nothing to worry about."

"You mean this isn't the first time they've pulled this?"

"I guess not. I didn't know about last year. If you need a witness I'll testify against them. I don't want to work for him anymore."

"Thanks, Sarah. Could you hang in there a few more weeks? As soon as I confront them with this, I'll be selling my share of the business. I want no more contact with either one of them."

As soon as Sarah hung up the phone, I called Robert Armstrong and dropped the forms off at his accounting firm.

Sam called me, "Will you be home this afternoon?"

When I told him, yes, he asked if he could stop by, "Only for a couple of hours. I think the rest of the week is going to be hectic and this may be the only chance for us to see each other."

A few minutes later Sam came in the kitchen door. He was drawn and tired, his usual look these days. The kidnapping case was taking a toll.

"How is the case developing?"

"Slowly, but there has been one interesting development, we now know who owns the Quonset hut."

"So you know who the kidnapper is?"

"No, the man who owns it is in a nursing home but his grand-daughter works for the history department at IUPUI."

I flashed back to the woman who said she drove Dr. Cutler when he needed a ride. Didn't he say she worked for the history department?

"She may be the woman I met when Dr. Cutler bought me the hot chocolate. And Doris dropped her books on his foot," I added, in case he had forgotten the incident. But, judging by his throbbing jaw, Sam remembered every detail.

"She's coming into the precinct this evening for an interview, that's why I want to spend time with you now."

Spending time with Sam made for a very enjoyable afternoon which is why I totally forgot to tell him about Henry's questions and his meeting with Dr. Fletcher.

Chapter 43

I didn't expect to see Sam for the next few days but he texted me the next morning. *Is it too early to stop by for coffee? I'll bring the bagels.*

While I made coffee, I asked, "How did your interview go last night?"

"The woman denied knowing anything about kidnapped students being kept in the Quonset hut. She said all she does is collect rents from the tenants who lease her grandfather's land. She has never seen the building and, as far as she knows, it's abandoned and will someday be torn down."

"Do you believe her?"

"I have no reason not to. Her story is entirely plausible…" He paused.

"Is there a 'but' Sam?"

"Yes. She didn't seem upset or shocked that someone was using the hut to hide kidnapped girls, and she was entirely too well prepared for our questions. Most people are nervous or have to think to remember every detail, but with her, it all tripped very easily off her tongue."

"What will you do?"

"We thanked her for her cooperation and she went away thinking we were done with her. In a few days we'll go to her workplace, take her to Shelbyville and start the questioning all over again, only this time the questions will be a lot harder."

"I have something to tell you that might have to do with what you're working on." I told Sam about my meeting with Henry and his interest in Sam's case. "He knew that five students had been kidnapped and that he, and the others, had not been looking for a stalker at school as they had been told. Doris was shocked. She'd said nothing to Henry about the kidnappings. Last night Doris and I had dinner at Luigi's and Henry was there with Dr. Fleming. He's another history professor at IUPUI. He teaches Ancient Greece. They had what looked like a cordial meeting, and when Dr. Fleming left, Henry followed him. Doris and I would have gone after them, but…" I stopped when I saw Sam's face. He was struggling to keep his anger under control, so I quickly said, "by the time we got to my car they had both disappeared."

I quickly changed the subject. "Jack asked me to come to the office to sign the annual tax forms. Robert Armstrong had advised me not to sign until he had checked them, which upset Jack and Andrew. I took the forms with me to give to Robert, despite Andrew's objections. Sarah, Jack's secretary called me soon after I left the office to tell me Andrew forged my signature and mailed it off anyway."

Sam frowned. "Cheating the IRS is a pretty serious business. I'm surprised your ex-husband was stupid enough to go along with the scheme."

"Sarah heard them talking. Andrew said they'd gotten away with it the year before and nothing would go wrong."

"So all this was Andrew's idea?"

"I think so. We've never liked each other too well. He disapproves of me as a mother-in-law and blames me for Ellie wanting a divorce. In any event, Jack went along with it."

"What an idiot. Let me know how it all works out." He finished his bagel, and topped off his coffee. "Looks as if my next interview will be with the history professor and then Henry."

He checked his watch and stood. Taking me in his arms, he held me tightly. "Kate, promise me you'll have nothing more to do with my case, no discussing it with anyone, no following people in cars. We're very close, I can feel it. Please, please stay out of it."

I didn't want to add to his stress, so I kissed him and promised.

Chapter 44

I decided to keep up the pressure and pay Jack another visit. Sarah told me he was alone and I waltzed into his office to find him sitting at his desk with his head in his hands.

He hastily stood. "Kate, what are you doing here today?"

"I thought I'd pick up the account books from last year for Robert to go over."

"Why?"

"Since you tried to cheat me out of a considerable amount of money this year, I thought I'd check last year's return. After all, you changed accountants half way through the year."

He tried the charm that used to work so well with me. "Kate, do you really think I'd deliberately try to cheat you? You know me better than that."

I was losing patience. "Enough with the lies, Jack. I want the books, both sets."

His face blanched. "I don't know what you're talking about."

"Then let me explain. You and Andrew have been keeping a double set of books. You can either let me have them or I'll contact the IRS and report you."

Jack was in shock but I went on, "Robert will determine how much money you have cheated me out of. You will file two amended returns, one for this past year and also for the year before and you will pay me every penny owed."

He tried to bluff his way through, "You have no proof whatsoever."

"On the contrary, I have copies of both of this year's books, and I know either you or Andrew forged my signature on the tax return and mailed it in."

"You can't possibly know that."

"Would you like to bet on it?"

I didn't want to get Sarah in trouble. She might need a reference one of these days, so I said, "I called your secretary to tell her it would be a few days before I could return the tax document and she told me it was signed and mailed."

"There's more, unless Andrew gives Ellie an equitable divorce with full custody of the twins, I will make sure he goes to prison for fraud. You will also lose your law license."

A speechless Jack sank into his chair his face as white as the papers I held in my hands.

He looked as if he were on the point of collapse but I was relentless, "I'm not leaving without the books."

He tried to say he didn't have the safe combination. I laughed, walked behind the desk and opened it myself. Speechless, he handed me what I wanted.

As I left, I turned to him, "I will not be in partnership with someone as unethical as you. I'm selling my half of the business."

"Kate. I can't afford to buy you out, right now."

"I didn't say I was selling to you, Jack."

"Kate, please. We built this business together. I made a mistake. I was angry. You wouldn't reconcile with me when I asked and you were dating that police detective. What was I to do? You had been my wife for thirty years."

"Which you forgot the moment the blond bimbo came to work for you."

"I was generous with you during the divorce."

"Only because you wanted it over with and were trying to avoid further scandal. You had visions of being on the school board and city council."

"At least give me time to get the money together. I only need a few months."

I leaned across the desk. "You let that worthless piece of trash Ellie is married to threaten her with losing her children, let him blackmail her into staying in a bad marriage, let him take every penny from her and did nothing to help her when she was desperate. And you expect leniency from me? No Jack, I'm selling my share of the business and you have no input on to whom."

He had his head on the desk almost sobbing. "Do our thirty years together mean nothing to you?"

I answered, "No." and left.

Chapter 45

I needed to think. I wandered over to the playing fields to calm myself. The wind was blowing the falling leaves into swirling piles and I strolled through them, kicking them aside until I came to the bench where I had sat with Henry.

It took a minute or two before I realized I was not alone. Someone was sitting on the other end of the bench. It was Henry and he held a photograph in his hand.

"Do you mind if I sit?"

The sound of my voice startled him and he dropped the picture. I quickly knelt down and picked it up. He snatched it from my hand but not before I had seen a laughing Henry with his arm around a young blond teenager. She was holding up a fish for the camera and they both looked happy.

He stowed it away in an inside pocket of his jacket and motioned for me to take a seat.

"Can you tell me if the police department is any closer to solving this case?"

It took me a moment before I realized he was talking about the kidnapped girls. "I'm sorry the only thing I know is that they feel as if they're getting close."

He was silent for a moment, then, "Mrs. Conley, you have grandchildren that you love?"

"Yes." I was surprised by his question.

"And no matter if they get to be fifteen or fifty you will still love them and would do anything to protect them?"

"Of course."

"What if you failed?"

I wasn't sure what he was trying to say, "I can't imagine."

He looked off into the far distance. There was an incredible sadness about him.

"I hope you never find out."

He made a visible effort to pull himself together. "Cherish the time you have with them. Goodbye, Mrs. Conley."

And he left me sitting on the bench alone. That was the last time I saw Henry.

Chapter 46

We had lost so much rehearsal time over the Bitch Barbara debacle that Sebastian was driving us extra hard. Consequently, I hadn't seen Sam for over a week, and I was pleasantly surprised to get a text from him asking if he could come over that evening. Of course, I said yes. Our rendezvous was delayed due to our after rehearsal custom of meeting up at the Pancake House. I would gladly have skipped it, but Doris loved going there, so I sat impatiently while everyone joked and laughed about silly, inconsequential things that had happened during rehearsal.

It took longer than usual. Sylvia was telling her favorite story which I had heard before—more than once. "Her line was 'She's on the verge of a nervous breakdown' but instead, during our first performance." Sylvia paused to take a breath. "And she said, 'she's on the nerve of a virgin's breakdown'—the audience was almost hysterical."

The whole table erupted into laughter and I dutifully joined in, maybe not as wholeheartedly as the rest of the crew and we were finally able to leave.

I dropped Doris off at her back door and hurried upstairs. Sam was in the shower. I slid into my side of the bed. A few minutes later the shower turned off. I heard his footsteps in the hallway. He almost collapsed into the bed. I turned to him only to be greeted by a soft snore. Sam was dead to the world.

The next morning he did redeem himself, which was why he only had time for a quick cup of coffee before dashing out of the kitchen door.

I wanted to tell him of the strange conversation with Henry but before I could say anything his phone rang. I heard him say, "Williamson"—then silence and a terse—"Be right there."

He turned back to me, "Gotta go—see you tonight, if I can."

And he went clattering down the stairs.

Before I even had time to get dressed, Doris was hammering on my door, "Kate, turn on the television. You have to watch the news."

I did as she asked, only to find the newscaster had switched to the weather and we had to go through the whole cycle again before the breaking news came back on.

While we were impatiently waiting, Doris kept up a non-stop flow of chatter, "Who would have thought it? Now what will you do about classes? I thought you were going to take both of his?"

I tried to stem the tide, "What are you talking about?"

Before she could answer, the news came back on and the anchor quickly put on her sad face, the one she used for serious events. "Dr. Neville Cutler, beloved IUPUI history professor committed suicide earlier today. His colleagues are devastated."

The story unfolded. Dr. Cutler had shot himself in the head in the early hours of the morning. No other details were released. Since school was out until the end of January there were few people on campus for the onsite reporter to interview, but he did his best. It wasn't much, simply the length of his tenure, details of his educational background and the usual thoughts and prayers.

Doris and I looked at each other.

Finally she said, "Well, who would have thought it? He seemed like such a nice man." Then she asked the question I was thinking. "Do you think this has anything to do with Sam's kidnapping cases?"

I had no answer.

Chapter 47

Apart from the occasional text, I didn't see or hear from Sam for three full days. I went to rehearsal, worked the morning shift at the library, but the whole time I was thinking about Dr. Cutler's suicide. There was nothing more in the media—the death of an obscure academic didn't rate much air time after the initial report. The school was holding a memorial service in two days and I was wondering if I should attend when Doris came knocking at my door with the answer.

"Kate, I think we should go to that teacher's funeral. The Oppenheims agree with me."

"Why would the Oppenheims want to go?"

She sighed. "Henry's no longer coming to the Senior Center. Nobody knows where he's disappeared to and it's getting boring now. We thought maybe he'd come to the funeral. He was always kinda interested in Dr. Cutler."

It was obvious Doris was planning on going. I didn't see how our attendance could impact Sam's case in any way; Dr. Cutler didn't have a car or even a driver's license so could hardly be one of his suspects. I agreed to go with her.

It wasn't a funeral, simply a very hurriedly put together, memorial service. It was held in one of the large auditorium classrooms in Cavanaugh Hall. A wreath of flowers decorated the stage. The room was barely half full and, as far as I could tell, it was mostly faculty with few students attending. Doris and I sat in the back so we could 'scope out the room' as Doris put it. The Dean of Students gave the eulogy. Dr. Cutler was lauded for his many years of service and the cause of his demise was studiously avoided. When invited, a few of the staff went up to the stage and shared a few remembrances with the crowd. Dr. Ted Thompson and Dr. Fleming were not among them. After the brief service, the mourners were invited to stay for refreshments and Doris was one of the first out of her seat for the cookies and punch line. I didn't want either, so I remained seated and waited for Doris.

Despite the hat which covered most of her face, I recognized the woman sitting in the row in front of me. It was Stephanie, Dr. Cutler's assistant, whom I had met the night Dr. Cutler bought me the hot chocolate and bored me to tears with his diatribe about the Black Death. She was dressed in heavy black and had spent most of the service with a wad of tissues pressed to her eyes which was why I hadn't identified her sooner.

When she got up from her seat to leave, I followed her and by hurrying ahead and then turning back towards the auditorium managed to almost bump into her.

"I'm so sorry." I pretended to just recognize her. "Oh, you're Stephanie, Dr. Cutler's assistant. What an awful thing to have happened. He must have been terribly depressed to do what he did."

She turned on me angrily. For a moment I thought she was going to hit me but, with a visible effort, she controlled herself. "He didn't do anything. Someone else shot him. I saw him that same night. He would never have killed himself—never." She roughly pushed past me and disappeared into the crowd.

When I got back to my seat, Doris was putting a plateful of cookies into one of the plastic bags she carried in her purse. "You want some of these, Kate.

They had plenty and these chocolate chips are really good."

As we left, I scanned the crowd. I didn't see the Oppenheims. Neither did I see Henry.

Chapter 48

Can I come up?

I was in the den watching television when Sam texted me. I'd already seen *Downton Abbey* at least a dozen times, so I turned off the television, texted him a *yes*, and met him in the living room.

After a brief hug, he held me away from him and asked, "Was there a reason you were at the memorial service today?"

I must have looked surprised because he went on, "He wasn't one of your teachers. I wondered why you were there."

"Sam, it had nothing to do with your case. You'd already told me he didn't drive and I know he bought me hot chocolate, but it wasn't drugged so he was hardly a suspect."

He was still looking at me with those piercing blue eyes of his, and I added, "Doris wanted to go because Henry seems to have disappeared and she thought he might be there."

"Was he?"

"No, but I did see Stephanie, Dr. Cutler's assistant. She told me that he wouldn't have committed suicide. I didn't ask," I said hastily, when Sam gave me the full force of his piercing eyes again. "I simply offered my condolences and that was what she told me."

I pulled him over to the couch and tried to change the subject, "Did you find out why Dr. Fleming had dinner with Henry?"

"Yes, Henry wanted to take one of his classes and was trying to decide which one and asked if they could meet for dinner."

"Did you believe him?"

"I accepted his explanation."

"But you didn't believe him."

Sam laughed. "Detectives don't believe or disbelieve. We keep plugging away, checking the facts until we finally arrive at the truth. Dr. Fleming has only been at IUPUI for two years."

"So he can't be the kidnapper because the first girl was kidnapped eight years ago?"

"Looks that way." Sam gave an enormous yawn and I gave up finding out anything more for that evening.

The only other piece of information I got out of Sam before he left the next morning was that Stephanie had claimed to be too distraught for an interview but, in light of what I had told him, he and Kevin were going to her home that afternoon.

"I'd like to know why she thinks he didn't commit suicide and I want to hear it before she can think up another story."

Winter storms were forecast with heavy snow expected by nightfall. The library was going to be short-staffed since Sebastian, Sylvia and Clarice would be at rehearsal that evening. My character wasn't in any of the scenes they were working on, so I volunteered for the evening shift to cover the shortfall. I was now hurrying to finish re-shelving the books lined up on the carts since it was almost certain the branch would be closed the next day. Due to the threatening weather, the building was almost devoid of patrons so it was easy for me to recognize someone I knew. As I looked over the balustrade from the upper level, I saw Dr. Fleming at the checkout counter. I drew back and watched as he checked out a couple of books. I'd never seen him at the library before.

I waited until he left then quickly ran down the stairs. "Wasn't that one of the history teachers at IUPUI?"

The clerk working the desk shook her head. "Don't know, love. My college days are long over."

"I think he's Dr. Fleming, teaches Greek history."

"Fleming? No, that wasn't the name on his card—it was something beginning with a T—Thomas or Thompson..."

Just then the closing announcement came over the speaker, the last of the stragglers brought their books over to be checked out and the clerk was too busy for further conversation.

I was halfway to the house before I remembered that Doris would be at the theater and I had nothing to eat at home. The maroon car following mine almost rear-ended me as I changed direction and turned right towards the deli on the square. The driver slammed on the brakes and fishtailed on the snow-covered street for half a block before regaining control. As I pulled into a vacant space in front of the deli, the car turned toward the rear parking lot and disappeared behind the building. There were few cars on the street and the dining room was almost deserted. It looked as if they were on the verge of closing.

"Do you have any food left?"

The girl behind the counter looked up from her phone long enough to say, "We only got baked chicken and some mashed potatoes."

"No vegetables or salad?"

She yelled towards the back of the counter, "Any vegetables left?"

A rough voice yelled back, "Got some broccoli."

"Broccoli would be fine." I shivered as a cold draft swirled around me. Someone must have opened an outside door somewhere. "Can I have a cup of coffee?"

She filled a cup with the dregs from the pot. "Cream and sugar over there." She gave a vague wave of her hand before gluing her eyes back to her phone.

I sat at a table near the side door to the parking lot and sipped the coffee. At least it was hot.

A disembodied voice from the nether regions of the deli bellowed, "We don't got broccoli no more."

I walked back to the counter as the young girl yelled towards the back again, "What else you got left?"

She turned to me, "He got collard greens."

"Collard greens will be fine."

I sat down at the table again and finished my coffee. The temperature was rising. I opened my coat and undid my scarf, but I was beginning to sweat. The deli started rotating like a giant kaleidoscope, throwing out flashes of sparkling light. I pushed back my chair and stood. I had to get outside before I threw up. A hand slid under my arm and helped me to the side door. The bitterly cold air briefly brought me back to full consciousness. I stumbled down the side of the building. There was a face next to me, but it was spinning around and kept changing. It was Dr. Fleming then it morphed into creepy Ted Thompson, then frail Henry, nonentity Henry, Darnley Henry and all the faces spun around in one giant merry-go-round before I disappeared into darkness.

I woke up in my own bed. My head was throbbing, my mouth dry. I was dressed in the same clothes I had worn to the library the night before. Doris was slumped in a chair by my bedside. She wore her old flannel robe and looked to be fast asleep with her head resting on her chest.

It was morning. I figured that much by the bright light coming in around the drawn curtains and I was ravenously hungry. *What had happened to me? Why was I still dressed?* I pressed my head into my hands in an effort to remember. *I worked my shift at the library and drove home. No, I remembered that Doris was going to be at rehearsal, so I stopped somewhere for food—the deli. Collard greens—there was something about collard greens and being dizzy.*

I tried to sit up and Doris woke with a start. "Kate, are you all right? I'll get you some tea."

"No, don't go. What happened to me?"

Tears filled her eyes. "I don't really know. You rang the back door bell and when I answered it you passed out."

"I rang the bell?"

I tried to recall the events of the previous evening, but could only get as far as deciding to go to the deli for food—there was nothing else except the collard greens.

"Yes..." she broke off, her hands were shaking. "Kate, I was so scared for you. You were unconscious. I called a doctor I know from the Senior Center, and she said you'd been drugged, but you'd be all right once you slept it off. She took a blood test and we called Sam."

She looked at me, her eyes full of concern. "Do you remember anything about last night?"

"Only that I worked at the library and stopped at the deli on the way home to get dinner for us both. After that there's nothing. What time did I get back here?"

"It was after midnight. I don't know the exact time—I was too shook to look at the clock. Your car was parked in the garage. Sam checked. But the doctor said there was no way you could have driven it yourself."

I tried to remember the previous night. I'd worked until the library closed at eight then drove straight to the deli. So I had to have arrived there before eight-thirty. That left over three hours unaccounted for. *What had happened in that time?*

"Does Sam know what happened?"

Doris shook her head and broke down into sobs.

I scrambled out of bed to comfort her and abruptly collapsed back on my pillows when a fit of dizziness swept over me. Doris hastily dried her eyes. "I'm all right now."

She left to make some tea for us. I crawled back into bed and promptly fell asleep.

Chapter 49

I awoke for the second time that day. I was still in yesterday's clothes, thirsty and hungry. Angry tones resonated from the kitchen. Sam was doing most of the talking.

The conversation abruptly ceased and I heard footsteps in the hallway. The bedroom door softly opened and Sam cautiously poked his head around it. He breathed a sigh of relief when he saw that I was awake.

"I didn't want to disturb you but…" He came closer to the bed and sat on the edge of it. He gently stroked the side of my face as his amazing blue eyes took in every detail. "Are you ready to talk about what happened?"

The door crashed open and Doris marched in carrying a heavy tray. "Move that table over next to the bed, Sam."

Sam jumped up to do her bidding as she went on, "Kate's not doing anything until she has some food inside her."

Sam stood by the side of the bed for a few minutes as Doris fussed around pouring my tea and making sure everything was within reach for me. The pulse in his jaw visibly throbbed. He finally strode toward the door. "I'll be outside shoveling snow. We'll talk when I'm done."

The tension in the room diminished and I was able to give Doris' lavish breakfast the attention it deserved, before taking a shower and changing my clothes. Sam returned. His cheeks were flushed from the cold and he was blowing on his hands to warm them. A silent Doris slid a cup of coffee in front of him and left the room.

Sam sat on the side of the bed. "What happened last night, Kate?"

"I don't really know. I worked the closing shift at the library because they were short handed. Doris was at rehearsal and I decided to stop at the deli on the Square to get dinner for both of us. They were on the point of closing and that's pretty much all I remember."

He was silent for a moment. "Anything happen at the library that raised a red flag?"

"No. We weren't busy, probably because of the storm that was blowing in." Then I remembered something. "I saw Dr. Fleming, the history teacher from school. He was checking out a number of books."

"Did he see you?"

"I don't think so. I happened to look over the banister and saw him at the checkout counter."

"Then you drove straight to the deli? Was it snowing yet?"

I put my face in my hands. *What had happened after that?* "I'm sorry, Sam. Yes, it was snowing. I turned suddenly and the car behind me almost ran off the road, it was so slick. When I got there, I must have parked, though I don't remember doing it. Something about collard greens sticks in my mind and that's all I remember."

"Collard greens?"

I nodded my head. There was more—I knew that, but it was gone, erased from my memory.

Sam held me gently. "Don't try to force it. Get some more sleep—we'll save the rest for a formal interview at the precinct. Something might come back to you in a couple of days."

He stood. "I've got to get back to work."

I walked with him into the kitchen. We heard the noisy scraping sound of a plow going down the alley behind the house. Sam rushed over to the window. "Damn it. I just cleared last night's snow from behind the garage and fence, now the plow's piled it back up. I'll have to do it all over again."

As soon as Doris heard the kitchen door slam, she sidled into the room. "Feeling better?"

I was. My headache had disappeared. I was comfortably full but still sleepy.

"Doris, why are you and Sam angry with each other?"

She shrugged her shoulders. "He wanted to take you to the emergency room, but I wouldn't let him."

"Because...?"

"The doctor was on her way. When she examined you, she said it would be better if you slept it off. Sam didn't agree. There was nothing more the hospital could have done for you. The doctor took a blood sample to see if she could find out what drug was used. He's still mad at me."

"Doris, who brought me home? The doctor said there was no way I could have driven but my car was in the garage."

She dropped her head and muttered, "Don't know."

"How did you get me upstairs and into bed if I was passed out?"

I saw the look of consternation on her face before she set her lips and answered me, "I managed. Kate, I already answered all these questions from Sam. I got work to do."

She left, slamming the kitchen door behind her. I was left wondering what she was hiding.

Chapter 50

The next couple of days passed in a pleasant fog. We had two more inches of snow and Vincent came over to help Rose and Enid clear the pathways and sidewalk. They could have waited. The temperature started to rise and we got, what was for Indiana, a winter heat wave.

By the time they were through shoveling, it had climbed into the mid-forties and the snow turned into slush.

Doris insisted I had to stay inside and rest, so I did my part by heating a big pot of ham and beans that I'd made in one of my rare cooking moods. That, plus cheese, grapes and a batch of Doris' biscuits made a perfect feast for our chilled workers and the five of us sat around my kitchen table enjoying being all together for once.

"Vincent, how is the job going for you?" Rose wanted to know.

"Great." The usually shy Vincent waxed enthusiastic. "I help out at the farm, too. I might move in there. Bert has plenty of room. Then he can rent out the apartment over the shop to bring in more revenue." He looked around the table. "What with his wife's medical bills and only being open three days a week, he lost a lot of business this past year. But it's starting to build up again. I've decided to go to grad school for my MBA then I can really help him."

He was silent for a moment then put his spoon down. "There is something I want to ask you."

Doris patted his hand. "You go right ahead, honey."

"When Bert visits his wife at the hospital, he takes me with him, and that's okay because she likes to see me. The only thing is she's started to call me David."

"Isn't that the name of her son, the one who was killed in the car accident?" *Which was the reason Ada Fletcher was in the mental institution*, I thought to myself.

"Yes, but what do you think about her calling me David?"

"What does Bertram think?" Doris wanted to know.

"He says it makes her happy, so it's okay."

"But it bothers you, right?"

"It seems dishonest."

Enid weighed in with her opinion. "Ada Fletcher's never going to get out of the mental institution—we all know that. If she's happy thinking you're her dead son, what's the harm?"

"It's only a couple of hours a week," chimed in Rose.

Vincent's face cleared. "I don't mind it, but I wanted to know what you all thought."

Doris waved a finger in his face. "It's a very kind thing to do for the poor woman. Let her have her delusion."

Sam came by the next morning just as Doris and I were sitting down to breakfast.

"I have something to tell you."

Doris immediately stood to leave, but Sam stopped her. "You may as well listen, too. It'll be public knowledge very soon."

She sat back at the table, but not before sliding a full platter and mug of coffee in front of him. Sam was forgiven!

Through a mouthful of biscuits and gravy, Sam started, "We interviewed Stephanie Morris, the History

Department's secretary, though I think she calls herself administrative assistant. You were right, Kate. She doesn't believe Cutler committed suicide. She thinks he was murdered."

"Is there any evidence of that?"

"Nothing that stood out. There was a suicide note on his computer saying he was sorry for everything, but gave no details—very generic. The gun's placement, the gunpowder residue on his hands, the blood spatter patterns are all consistent with a suicide. It's still an open case until we get the autopsy results which won't be for a couple of weeks, but there's nothing suspicious about this."

Doris was making a visible effort to remain quiet. She lost the struggle and blurted out, "What about the kidnapped girls?"

Sam smiled to himself and went on, "The woman broke down completely when I asked her if she felt that Dr. Cutler's death and the kidnappings were connected. That's when she said they were the reason for his supposed murder and then it all came pouring out."

He pushed the plate, whose contents he had virtually inhaled, away from him, took a long swig of his coffee and continued, "She had driven Dr. Cutler to school that day and he seemed agitated. Scared was the word she used. When she drove him home that evening, he wanted her to come in, which was unusual, but she said he wanted to talk."

"He told her that about eight or nine years ago, he and Dr. Ted Thompson were at a farewell dinner for a colleague. They got roaring drunk together and the retiring professor told them that he had one wish unfulfilled. When they asked what it was, he said he always wished he could get rid of problem students by dumping them in the back of beyond and making them find their own way out."

"Cutler said, at the time he and Ted Thompson laughed about it, and promptly forgot they'd ever had the conversation. A couple of months later, Ted Thompson came to him. He told Cutler he had a student who was constantly challenging him in class and was disruptive. He told him that he was going to implement their plan. Stephanie insists Cutler thought it was a joke until the student disappeared and was found the next day wandering around the countryside dazed and confused. She promptly quit school. A year later, Thompson did it again. Cutler told her no harm came to the girls. They both were found the next morning and Thompson bragged to him that he got rid of two problem students. He even took Cutler out for a celebratory dinner."

"Then Cutler had a problem. As you know, he taught British history and liked to brag about his time spent teaching at Oxford—a major English university."

"I know what Oxford is, Sam. But Dr. Cutler never taught there," Doris eagerly interjected.

Sam smiled at her. "Good catch. How did you know?"

Doris beamed; the feud was over. "Henry told me."

Sam raised an eyebrow and went on, "He had taught in the UK, but it was at a minor university near Sheffield. Unfortunately for Cutler, this student had taken a summer course at Oxford and was well acquainted with the college and town. She asked a lot of questions about his time there, and also challenged him on some of his glaring errors in topography and descriptions of local watering holes, when he came up with his Oxford anecdotes. He was furious and complained to Thompson, who said it would be easy to get rid of the problem. Thompson drugged the girl with spiked coffee from the cafeteria and Cutler drove her a few miles east on I-74 and dumped her in some woods close to the highway. Stephanie said that Cutler just wanted to scare her enough that she would quit school, but things went horribly wrong. It was early November, temperatures dropped, there was a freak snowstorm that night and the student died of hypothermia. Cutler was distraught. He gave up driving, sold his car and that was the end of the kidnappings until Fleming came on the scene."

"The Greek history professor?"

"Yes."

"Did Stephanie already know about the kidnappings?"

"Only the later ones, Kate, not the first three. She's not sure how Fleming learned about them, but he became close friends with Ted Thompson who might have told him. Fleming threatened Cutler with exposure unless he helped him."

Doris was on the edge of her seat. "So that Greek history teacher is involved? You think Henry figured it out and that's why he had dinner with him?"

Sam rose from his seat and paced the floor restlessly. "We're not sure what Henry's role is in all this. Anyway, the Stephanie woman will be facing charges. She had to have told Fleming about the Quonset hut. She says she had no idea he was hiding the kidnapped students there, but Cutler knew and he probably told her."

"So if Cutler didn't drive, what did he do?"

Doris almost raised her hand, she was so eager to answer me. "He was the one who drugged the girls."

"You're right. The last two girls were from Thompson's class. Thompson complained to Fleming, and Fleming decided to do Thompson a favor. He told Cutler who they were and Cutler waited for the right opportunity to slip them the rohypnol. She thinks Fleming transported them. Stephanie said Fleming did it for laughs. But chaining young women up in a deserted hut makes him the most dangerous of the three. He was the one who dumped the first girl, Claire. She almost died of exposure and the second girl could have had an asthma attack. There are a lot of blanks to fill in but that can wait until we interview Fleming and Thompson."

"When will that be?" I asked.

"Don't know. They both seem to have disappeared."

Chapter 51

After Sam left, Doris helped me clear the breakfast dishes from the table. Digger took care of the floor. I was expecting her to leave as soon as the dishwasher was loaded, but she seemed reluctant to go.

Finally she sat back at the table. "Kate, there's something I have to tell you. I'm hoping you won't tell Sam, but I'll understand if you feel you have to. Anyway, I don't think he's coming back."

"Who?"

She sighed. "Henry. He's the one who drove you home and carried you upstairs the night of the snowstorm."

"Why did you lie to me and Sam?"

"Henry told me to. Kate, I owed him that much. Those two teachers drugged you and were going to kidnap you. Henry was following your car and he managed to stop them."

I thought for a moment. "Did he say why he was following me?"

"No, but he must have thought you were in some kind of danger. He told me he'd taken care of the problem and it wouldn't happen again. I asked him how and he said it's best if I don't know."

"Doris, my car was in the garage, right?"

She nodded.

"Who put it there?"

"Henry."

"But he was driving his own car that night. So who was driving mine?"

There was a sharp intake of breath. "You're saying he had help?"

"He must have. Who could it have been?"

The answer came slowly, "I don't know."

But I think she did.

Chapter 52

Two days went by before Sam asked me to call in at the precinct for a formal interview about the night I was drugged, and then rescued, by Henry.

As soon as I walked into the squad room, I knew something else had happened. Detectives Hanley and Kreutz were huddled together with Sam and engaged in an intense conversation. They broke off and separated when they saw me.

Hanley opened the door to the interview room, "Sam, you might as well sit in. Whatever Kate tells us now is redundant."

Redundant? What was that supposed to mean?

Kreutz asked the first question, "Mrs. Conley, do you remember anything more about the night of the kidnapping?" He added, "Sam, filled us in on what happened to you."

"Only that when I worked at the library that evening Dr. Fleming came in and checked out some books. He used Ted Thompson's card."

"That makes sense if he needed an excuse to visit the library," Sam interjected. "He doesn't live in Shelby County, so wouldn't have had a library card."

"But Thompson does?"

Kreutz replied to my question, "Yes, he lives in Pleasant View, just over the Marion County line. Did you see Fleming after he checked out his books?"

"No, but a car followed me when I left the library. It was a maroon color. That's the same as Dr. Fleming's car."

I leaned across the table and looked at the three of them, "Was Fleming the one who drugged me and took me out of the deli?"

Kreutz nodded. "We can't be sure. The young girl behind the counter didn't see you leave."

"That's not surprising; she had her eyes glued to her phone the whole time I was there..." I stopped. I had just remembered the girl in the deli.

"I remember that I felt sick and dizzy so I hurried outside before I threw up. Someone helped me." The hand under my elbow—the events of that night were coming back to me. "Everything started going around and around and I woke up in my own bed."

Sam frowned. "Doris says someone—it couldn't have been you—rang the doorbell at midnight which means there are three hours unaccounted for. Do you remember anything that happened during those three hours?"

I thought hard. "At one point, I think I was in the back seat of a car. I remember the motion of the car but I'm not sure and it was only a brief flash of memory."

The three men looked at each other then Sam spoke, "The case is now closed. Fleming and Thompson were found early this morning, in a wooded area close to I-74, a few miles from Shelbyville. They had ingested a lot of alcohol and must have been drinking until they passed out. There were four empty whiskey bottles at the site. They both died of hypothermia."

Hanley spoke up, "By a strange coincidence, the student that Cutler kidnapped, who also died of hypothermia, was found in almost the exact location."

I was confused. "So are you saying that Thompson and Fleming were the ones who drugged and kidnapped me?"

There was silence.

"Doris says that Henry was the one who brought me home?"

The three men looked at each other again. A pulse was throbbing in Sam's jaw, so I hastily added, "Doris says that Henry asked her to not tell anyone."

Kreutz cleared his throat. "Henry has disappeared. His car was found a few miles from here, almost totally destroyed by fire."

"But you think he was involved?"

Sam answered, "Since he was the one who brought you home, he had to have been. Why, we don't know. We have no idea who he is. He told everyone that he worked for the government in a low-level security job, but his fingerprints aren't in any database. Fleming's car was found covered in snow and abandoned in a rest stop near where they were found. We had the idea of looking in the same location where the dead student was found, all those years ago, and that's where they both were."

My head was reeling. "Are you saying that we'll never know what happened?"

"According to the secretary, Thompson and Cutler were responsible for the first three kidnappings and the death of one of those students. The other two students were kidnapped by Fleming and Thompson with help from Cutler. Your attempted kidnappings were by the same three except Cutler, again according to Stephanie Morgan, had an attack of conscience and couldn't go through with it the second time. He was already dead when they tried again."

Kreutz continued, "We've been told by our superior to close out the case. The kidnappings will be officially unsolved. Cutler's death will be a suicide. Fleming and Thompson's deaths will be an accident brought on by excessive alcohol and depression over the death of a friend."

"What we can't figure out," said Hanley, "is why this Henry, who must have had some security background, would involve himself in this. And who helped him? There's no way he could have rescued Kate, dumped two bodies out in the boonies, brought her and her car home and set fire to his own car alone. Logistically, he had to have had help."

Kreutz spoke up again, "I don't care that those three guys are dead. They were sickos and eventually their violence would have escalated. What is really bugging me is why someone, who has to have had a high security clearance, would be involved?"

Sam shook his head. "Accept it. Justice has been served even if it's vigilante justice. Think of the paperwork it saves us."

It was time for me to leave. Sam and his colleagues had a lot more to discuss.

As I passed through the squad room, Kevin was taking down the white board and photographs of the kidnapping case. I looked at the five victims and one photo caught my eye. It was of the third victim, the one who had died of hypothermia. It showed a high school graduation photo of a beautiful young woman displaying her high school diploma. I had seen her before. She was older in this picture, but I recognized her from the snapshot Henry had inadvertently dropped at my feet the last time we met. She was the laughing teenager, pictured with her arm around him, proudly holding her fish for the camera.

I said goodbye to Kevin and left. Henry's secret was safe with me.

Epilogue

Everyone agreed it was a beautiful wedding. The old stone building next to the winery was festooned with purple and lilac flowers. White bows decorated the ends of each aisle. The mother and grandmother were resplendent in lilac dresses and all the groomsmen had purple bow ties and boutonnieres. Sam was almost as radiant as the bride as he walked the beautiful, glowing Mira down the aisle.

Our little twins performed their duties admirably except for one minor glitch when, halfway to their destination they decided for some reason known only to themselves, to swap the satin cushions holding the wedding rings. The rings reached their destination safely and, mission accomplished, the boys scampered back to where Ellie, Doris, Martha and I sat. They watched the rest of the ceremony in wide-eyed wonder.

It was a text book wedding, Sam danced with Mira and halfway through handed her off to her step-father. The toasts were given, the cake was cut and everything was perfect until it came time for the throwing of the bridal bouquet.

We all gathered together and somehow Ellie and Martha dragged me through to the front of the crowd. A laughing Mira turned her back to us. Ellie and Martha hemmed me in until the last second, and as the bouquet sailed through the air and descended, stepped away. Doris, who was standing immediately behind me, pushed me forward and the flowers fell into my outstretched hands.

A big cheer went up from the crowd. Mira clapped her hands in delight. Ellie and Martha hugged me. On the other side of the room, Kevin, Hanley and Kreutz thumped a laughing Sam on the back. The whole room was whooping and hollering. The only person not deliriously happy seemed to be me.

THE END

ABOUT THE AUTHOR

Trisha Durrant was raised in post-war Britain. After seeing an ad in the *London Times*, which said, 'Come to the sun-drenched desert of Arizona,' she immediately decided to emigrate. In her defense, it was raining at the time and she was an out of work actor who was tired of waiting on tables. Now, four children, eight grandchildren and too many cats to enumerate, later, she lives in the beautiful mountains of Madison County, North Carolina, with her remaining cat, Monty, nicknamed 'The Monster.' *Captive in the Quonset Hut* is the third book in her Kate and Doris Mystery series.

List of books by the same author.

Almost Abducted

Body in the Barn

Captive in the Quonset Hut

www.ingramcontent.com/pod-product-compliance
Lightning Source LLC
Chambersburg PA
CBHW020317260626
47156CB00004B/1255